Acknowledgements

I would like to first thank God for everything he has done and will continue to do for me. When I felt like giving up on life, he pulled me through and with each passing day I m getting stronger and stronger. To my mother Nellie Best, you are a ride or die lady. All I have to do is say, I need or I want and you are on it. Thank you for always being there for me. To my father Melvin Hester, I would like to thank you for being there for me especially these last couple of years. I m so glad we have gotten over the past and are now working on the kind of relationship I ve always wanted to have as a little girl.

My children Bryan Majette, Ashlie Majette, Marketa Salley and Andrea Thomas . how did I get so lucky to have children who love and support me as much as you guys do? Love you to pieces.

Jackie Davis...whew! Where do I begin? You are the epitome of what a real friend is. I don t care what time of day I call you you re there. Hell, you ve beat me in an ambulance to the hospital! Lol You re more than a friend, you re my sister. Love you! Speaking of sister, Shelly Majette Carrington, I don t know what I would do without in you my life. I can always count on you to tell me like it is and encourage me when I m feeling down. To my brothers Ronald and Melvin Williams, Kevin Levy and Equan Harley, my sister-in-law Keisha Williams, Marc Salley, Brandi Salley, Betty Hamilton and my God Father Earl Taylor, I thank you guys for your support and love. It really means the world to me.

To Tressa Smallwood, thanks for keeping the door open for me during my hiatus. You won t be disappointed! To Leslie Allen, Tasha Simpson, Virginia Greene, and the rest of the LCB crew, it has been a pleasure working with you guys and I look forward to our future projects. Thank you to Kellie with Dzine by Kellie for the hot cover!

There have been so many people who have supported me and been there for me in both my professional and personal life. I appreciate you more than you will ever know. With that said, I would like to give a shout out to my Aunts: Yvonne Tulley, Pauline Williams, Lucy Bailey, Wilma Johnson, Christine Majette, Katrina & Shanique Majette and Belinda Outlaw. Uncles: Johnny Majette, Wendell Majette, Stanley Majette, Darnell Drummond. Cousins: Shawn Carrington Sr., Keisha Majette, Dante Majette, Johnny Majette Jr., Neco Majette, Gwanda Majette, Toni Majette, Zenobia Majette, C.J. Majette, Latisha Russell, Elgen Majette, Bambi Curtis, Nicole Wiggins, Allen Bailey, Wanda Harrington, Jayda Flood, Jabria Carrington, Felicia Taylor, Shawn (Pud) Carrington Jr., Tarmara Readdy, Jamica Jenkins, Mike Majette Sr., Mike Majette Jr., Michele Nichols, Denise Nichols, Taneja Nichols, Wendy Nichols, Ty Hester, Mike Hester, Iceese Wesley. Nephew: Emmanuel Poobie Chapman and my niece Melkeda Williams, I love you more than words can say.

To my girls, Sheena Smith, Vace Evans and Sabrina Wright-Young, we had some good times back in the day. So glad that we ve managed to remain good friends after 20 years, because, as you know, we had to kick a few of them winches out of the circle! LOL

My Ace Laron Profit, Malik Savage of the *Let It Flow Band*, Violette Rice-Assenza, Nicole Rochelle, Danie Thomas, Michelle Butler, Travell Williams, Necole Salley, Noelle Salley, Linda Salley, Davon and Marty Salley, Andrea Doyle, Michelle Davis, Tiffany Stokes-McCaskill, Sasha Brown, Rosa-Carmen Agusta, Chypes Harrell, Marilyn Stone, Mandi Rounds, Kelly Gordan, Victoria Lewis, Yvette Bethea, Mike Kenney, Ayana Knight, Cheryl Bruce, Joyce Tillery, Candida Pinkett, Michelle Parham, Micheal Bim Kendrick, Alicia Moore, Lucion Freeman, Super Producer Bink Harrell, D.C. Councilman Sedrick Muhammad, Gospel Artist James Kelly Fox Davis, Kim, Lex and Dominique Brunson, SSH Photography and my cover model, the lovely Miss Mecca.

To my friend, Craig *Chedda Diamondz* Scott from Queens, NY, I m a true believer that God puts people in your life for a reason. I can t wait to give you a big hug. By the way, when you come home you owe me a new Gucci bag and dinner at Benihana! LOL

To party promoters, Jeff Robinson from Dynasty Five, Ron- Te Thomas from Se7en Productions, Maybach Marv, Sean Spencer from Velvet Entertainment, thank you for allowing me to set up tables at your events to promote my work.

To Ms. Joann Davis and Mr. Sherlock McDougal at Shaw University, I can t thank you enough for always going above and beyond to help me. Your dedication to the students of Shaw University is something that sets you apart from the rest. You are truly an asset to our school.

To all of the veterans and military service men and women who have served and are serving this country, I salute you. We are truly in a league of our own. Semper Fi!!!

Smooches,

Danette Majette

P.S. Follow me!
Instagram: @dcmajette @lcbooks
/Facebook: Danette Majette

 One...

I was so tired of being married to this mothafucka. I wanted somebody to explain to me why I did it. He's never treated me the way a lady should be treated, and acted like a bitch every time I wanted to go out. Of course, when his ass wanted to go out it was all good though.

"You not going nowhere, Zsaset!" Deonte shouted!

"You must be crazy," I returned while dabbing bronzer on my cheeks.

"I'm serious. Fuck that! Try being a wife sometimes."

My neck swiveled away from the mirror, and I dropped my make-up bag on the counter. "Shut the fuck up, Deonte! Maybe if yo' ass had some damn friends to hang out with, you wouldn't always be tripping off me and my friends." I found myself screaming at the top of my lungs.

Deonte had that ferocious look in his eyes that I knew all too well. He pounced around the house in a frenzy throwing jabs at the wall trying to intimidate me. It wasn't working. We had been arguing since Brina called and asked me to go to a party up in Richmond with her, Sheba and Nicole.

"Look, I'm going out and there's nothing you can do about it."

"Oh yeah," he snapped.

"You deaf or something?" I countered, letting him know

I still wasn't and had never been a punk.

Deonte started coming towards me with a vengeance. His fear tactic didn't work but I wasn't crazy either. He was a big nigga, two hundred and thirty pounds. At 6'3 he towered over my 5'4 slim, frame. His muscular arms could send me flying to the other side of the room easily so I grabbed my 5 lb. weight off the floor by my bed.

Up to this point, Deonte had only man-handled me. He hadn't actually hit me during our three years of marriage, but had a new-fangled look on his face. I knew things were about to get ugly, the way he balled his fists at his side. When I thought Deonte was in striking distance, I broke bad and swung with all I had. Unfortunately, my missed attempt sent my body spinning. Deonte took the opportunity to grab me by my hair, yanking me close to him. Out of the corner of my eye, I saw Zeta, our three year old, standing in the bedroom doorway holding her Barbie doll. I figured Ryan, my son from a previous relationship was pretending to be asleep. He hated it when we fought and often put a pillow over his head to drown out the yelling. Although, he was six, he'd told me countless times how much he wanted us to move away from Deonte.

He truly feared him.

"Get up!"Deonte shouted at me, as he tightened the grip on my hair. "Zsaset, your trifling ass can't ever act like a wife and a good mother. You are fuckin' twenty-five years old acting like you seventeen. My mother said your ass was trash. Look at your daughter standing over there…You think she proud of your trifling ass, Zsaset? Huh?"

I looked over at Zeta who stood there looking like the spitting image of her father; rich, caramel skin and all. The tears welling up in her eyes disturbed me. I begged her to go back to bed but she didn't move. In a weird sort of way she wanted to see how I would handle things.

"Answer me, Zsaset!"

Deonte said that same shit every time we argued. His grip on my hair was causing my head to throb in pain, but I managed to say, "Do you think I give a fuck what your mother thinks? She gave birth to a fucking pig!"

My words infuriated him. Deonte and his mother were very close so insulting her made the situation even worse. He gave me a slap across the face which immediately made me black out on his ass. It didn't matter to me that Zeta was still standing there.

"Get the fuck off me!" I yelled, as I pulled my small Swiss army knife out of my pocket and nicked him with it. He released my hair and looked down at his arm. While his attention was diverted, I kicked him in his sack. The moment he doubled over in pain and released my hair, I screamed down at Deonte.

"You ain't my fucking father, bitch!"

"You need some help, bitch!" he spat, squirming across the floor.

"Well, I'll get it on my way to the club."

I turned to Zeta and told her to stop crying. I assured her like the many times before that everything would be all right. It wasn't uncommon for her father to argue me down about my late nights out, especially since I was liable to hang out Sunday through Saturday. The only reason that I had been in the house the last couple of weeks was because I'd been sick as hell and my mother, who was my steady sitter had been out of town visiting my uncle in North Carolina.

I was also semi-depressed from conjuring up old feelings about being dishonorably discharged from the Marine Corps. Being in the military was the one thing in life that had my self-esteem on high. Enlisting at the age of eighteen turned out to be the best decision I'd ever made in life. But after assaulting my bitchy staff sergeant with a knife it all came to an end.

At the time, I'd only been dating Deonte for about three months so he was showering me with gifts, and wining and dining me. Lisa, my staff sergeant was obviously jealous. She was always putting me on shitty details and talking to me about

3

using protection so I wouldn't have any more kids out of wed-lock. The bitch got smart with me daily until I couldn't take it anymore. So after only being in the military for three years, I stabbed the hoe. At my court martial, I was found guilty and was almost sent to the brig, but my uncle who was a Colonel per-suaded them to just make me pay a hefty fine and discharge me.

I'd now gone from having a salary and benefits to hourly pay, working at the Exchange.

What a life?

And, oh, did I mention my marriage sucks?

Marriage hadn't slowed me down one bit and as a matter of fact, it sped me up. I got married too young and I wasn't happy. I ran the streets to avoid Deonte. Our relationship was falling apart. It was no surprise, considering we only dated three months before I got pregnant. We tied the knot shortly there-after. Deonte was a romantic and I got caught up in the fairytale. The fact that his family had a little money didn't hurt either. He had pretty chocolate skin and a smile to die for. But a few weeks after we were married, we were at each others' necks because we never got to know one another.

Besides…he was a Marine for sure and obsessive com-pulsive in every way.

Everything had to be in order and on time. That shit drove me crazy. By the time we realized that we weren't in love, it was too late. He was controlling and boring and I wasn't Holly the Homemaker. Hell, I didn't even like his sex that much, which drove him crazy. That's when I started hanging out with my girls every chance I got, which was almost every day.

Deonte's grumbling from the back bedroom snapped me back to reality. It was time for me to jet. Zeta was still crying at the doorway. I felt a twinge of guilt about leaving her upset so I consoled her by promising to take her to see Grandma the next day. I quickly gathered my party gear and rolled out before De-onte regained his composure. I could still hear him moaning as I left the room.

I pulled into Brina's complex at top speed. She was my

girl from way back. We'd been tight from the days of Tidewater Park Elementary and Mr. Collin's fourth grade class. She was the prettiest girl in our neighborhood and her mother always bought her designer clothes from New York that no one else in our neighborhood had. Those that didn't hate her, hated me because she liked me so much. People would always try to break up our friendship by telling us that the other one was talking about the other, but we never fell for their games. In fact, it made us closer.

I threw my car in park and blew the horn. I looked out the passenger side window and noticed Nicole talking to this guy who was wearing a North Face jacket. It was the same guy she had met in the Palace, a club we frequented downtown. We made eye contact and she put her finger up to me. I blew the horn so Sheba and Brina would come down. I sat in the car for about ten minutes finalizing my make-up before I yelled, "C'mon y'all, let's go!"

Patience was never one of my strong suits. Not to mention, I was ready to get my groove on and get out of Norfolk. I beginning to be so boring living there. After a few minutes, Brina and Sheba ran down the stairs and they all piled into the car. Before I could even drive two blocks, Sheba, who we called Rump Roast, lit up a blunt.

"Bitch, can't you at least wait until we get on the bridge!" I yelled, rolling down the windows.

In between long puffs on the blunt, Sheba slowly said, "Oh, I thought we were already on the bridge."

I laughed so hard, I had to pull over and get out of the car. When the four of us got together, it was always one big comedy show.

After we drove across the Hampton Roads bridge, Sheba rolled down the window and shouted, "Richmond, the Norfolk Divas are on their way, so get your money right, and make sure y'all clothes are on point!"

Sheba was a piece of work. For her, it was all about money, and men with money. She was the type of scandalous bitch you would have to sleep with one eye open around. She would fuck your man and smile in your face like it was nothing. I met Sheba through Brina about two years ago. We probably wouldn't have liked each other except for the fact that we were both tight with Brina. Sheba was cute, busty with broad shoulders and a big ass. She had the classic V-shaped body. Her dark pie shaped face sported thin lips and a flat wide nose. She dressed her ass off though and walked with confidence. If Sheba saw a dude she wanted, she approached him without hesitation. Most guys seemed turned on by her aggressiveness. Brina was the exact opposite. She was just as beautiful but she was the laid back type. She was a red bone with spiked blonde hair, and thick body that made her standout in a crowd. She was beyond beautiful on the inside and the outside.

"So Brina, who are these niggas we're going out with?" I asked.

"You remember K-Dog and his friends who came down a week ago?"

"Oh, the guys who went with us to the club?"

"Yeah, Boy, that's them," Brina said. For some crazy reason, Brina called everyone Boy.

"They look like ballers," Sheba said. "Although some niggas can fake it if you don't pay close attention."

"You would know best," I teased.

"Anyway," Brina interrupted. "They said if we came up they would take us out and show us a good time. All the Ace of Spades and food we want. Of course, everything's on them."

"That's my girl," Sheba said.

"Yeah, that's cool, as long as they ain't looking for no ass," I said.

Sheba rolled her eyes. "Speak for yourself, Zsaset."

"Look, just because you're known to "fuck for a buck" doesn't mean we will," I snapped.

"Look, we ain't come up here for all that. We're here to have fun. We just gonna go to the club, get our drink on and then bring our black asses back home," Brina said. "Oh, and I might back this ass up on K-Dog for a couple hours if he let me. He kinda stingy with his shit."

We all laughed, then she got quiet thinking about how pressed she sounded. After a few seconds of silence Brina added, "And we ain't looking for no drama tonight." We all looked at Nicole.

"What! Why y'all lookin' at me?" Nicole was notorious for starting shit. She took a long puff on the joint. In a low voice muffled by the joint's smoke, Nicole said,

"I'm chillin', I'm chillin' as usual."

I stared at Nicole with my eyebrow raised. Every fiber of my being told me that this wasn't going to be the fun-filled trip we thought it was going to be. Just before we got to Richmond, my cell phone started to ring. When I saw my home phone number displayed across the screen I started to send it to voicemail. Then I thought, What if it's an emergency with one of the kids?

Quickly, I answered. "Hello."

"Hi Mommy," Ryan said softly.

"Hi baby. What's wrong?"

"Deonte is doing that thing again."

My heart began to beat rapidly while the car began to swerve. "What is he doing?" I snapped.

"Being mean. Doing what you told him not to do."

Ryan went on to tell me Deonte was yelling at him because he was taking too long in the bathroom. He told him to stop shitting, get off the toilet and get back in the bed.

Angrily, I told him to give the phone to Deonte then I commenced to cursing his ass out.

"Just because Ryan isn't you're biological child doesn't mean you have to treat him like shit. Plus, you now Child Protective Services is watching you, damn it."

"That lil' nigga is a pussy! He's six years old still telling his momma everything!"

"Look, I told you before that if we ever have a repeat of what you did before there would be Hell to pay! And I fucking

7

mean it!"

"Well, then bring your ass home and watch him your-self," he said. He was right but I really didn't give a flying fuck.

I was used to him getting mad but he was really extra with it tonight. After going back and forth for a few minutes debating who the worst parent was, I heard a child screaming, then he hung up on me.

For the first time I felt bad about leaving my kid. Maybe my mother was right. Was I really waiting on something bad to happen before I turned my life around?

two...

By the time we got to Richmond, Sheba and Nicole were high as shit. Brina and I had a nice contact high because we kept the windows rolled up. We pulled up to Bar Louie's on Broad Street and couldn't believe our eyes. There were niggas all over the place. If you wanted a man this was the place to be. Especially if you wanted a New York dude; their swagger and impeccable taste in clothing made your average guy from down south look like a clown.

"Oh my God. I'm in heaven," Sheba said.

"It's more like hell for your devilish ass," I snarled.

As we circled the parking lot blasting reggae, Brina spotted K-Dog's 6 series BMW Coupe. "Pull in between the black Lexus truck and the white Audi," she said.

Brina stepped out of my Chrysler 300 and put on her sexy strut as she went over to greet K-Dog who was in Gucci, looking like Money Mayweather, except for the fact that he was much taller than Floyd. She'd told us they'd never fucked but her body language told me differently. He was a decent looking guy, who appeared to be a lot older than us...maybe mid-thirties. But he had major swag though. Brina previously confessed that K-Dog had been in and out of jail a lot, so tattoos suffocated his body. She wasn't exaggerating; I'd counted five, covering his neck and arms, but didn't want to stare too hard.

The next thing I knew, K-Dog's boys from New York were peeling out of the cars one by one sporting Prada, Louis Vuitton, Burberry and Hermes. We looked at each other like we had just hit the jackpot, and gave each other high-fives.

"Girl, I'm waiting for the ugly one to peel out. You know there's always that one ugly guy," I said.

"Not tonight. I guess they told his ass to stay home," Nicole said. "Ain't that the truth?"

We waited a few minutes, and then got out of my car. Brina introduced everyone except me. I knew it was her way of letting them know that I was "off limits". I cut in and cut my eyes at Brina, "And she forgot me, I'm Zsaset."

I heard the short, chubby guy they called Quan say under his breath, "Yeah, don't forget Zsaset."

Damn right, I thought to myself.

"So, you ladies ready to go clubbing?" K-Dog asked.

"Hell yeah," Sheba said.

K-Dog put his hands up and shouted, "Let's do it!" We got in the car and headed towards the club.

We drove about a mile before we reached the club. The line was wrapped around the comer. Mansion was the hottest club in Richmond and with DJ Lucky Lou on the turntables it was almost impossible to get inside on a Saturday. "I'm not standing in that long ass line to get into a club. It's too damn cold out here!" I yelled.

"Don't worry, K-Dog has connections here," Brina said.

"I hope so or I'll see y'all back in Norfolk."

We parked about a block from the club and started walking. I guess people could tell we weren't't from Richmond because all eyes were on us. And they had a reason to be, because our clothes were from high end boutiques like "Hush". I kept it simple with an Alexander McQueen top and a pair of Rag and Bone boyfriend jeans. My girls were equally fly. We all did different things to make money. I worked 40 hours a week and had access to Deonte's money whenever I wanted. Brina had her own T-shirt line called "I Love Labels" while Sheba and Nicole ran credit card scams for a living. They were both greedy so they fell out every other week. One thing we did have in common was we were all sexy as hell.

Being the divas we were, we sashayed down the sidewalk towards the door like it was all about us. But as usual, Nicole started getting irate when she saw these girls looking at us and whispering to each other.

"What the fuck y'all bitches lookin' at? Y'all must wanna get fucked up or somethin'."

Of course, I started laughing. I knew it was only a matter of time before she blew up. Come to think of it every time we got into some bullshit it was because of her. She hated a lot of things but more than anything else, she hated people staring at her. Nicole had a terrible attitude and the ability to fight like a heavyweight champ. She was a time bomb waiting to blow.

To make matters worse, Nicole was your classic pretty girl. She had light golden brown flawless skin, with light brown eyes to match. Nicole had that "I got Indian in my family" hair. It was long, wavy and cold black. She had an hour glass shape with a flat stomach and an ass like a shelf. Niggas loved her, though she didn't trip off of them too much. The average bitch disliked Nicole before she ever opened her mouth. Females wanted to whoop her ass just on G.P., but Nicole's shit talkin' always fueled the fire. She always assumed any off the wall comment someone mad they were referring to her. If she saw two girls talking and they just happen to look at her-well then they must've been talking about her. And God forbid you stop having a conversation when she walks up. She would lose it. Nicole was just paranoid like that but we loved her crazy ass anyway.

Brina put her arms around Nicole's shoulders and said, "Don't forget, Boy, we in these bitches' backyard."

"I don't give a fuck," Nicole shot back. But she must have thought about it because she wasn't that loud. I looked back at the girls standing in line. Just as I did, the little short fat one of the group said to her friends, "That's okay, we'll see that bitch inside."

We got to the front of the club, and security let us right in. "I told you he got connections," Brina said.

I guess he did. We got in for free, and we didn't even have to show our ID's.

In the club, K-Dog and his friends ordered about ten bottles of Rose'. The DJ was killing it. He was playing a mix version of Iggy Azalea's 'Fancy' that had everyone on the floor. I noticed K-Dog's friend named O.B staring at me. I had actually scoped him out from the moment he got out of K-Dog's car. He was about 6' 1, slim with a rock hard body, and a fashion sense that made him even more appealing to the eye. He was dressed in a pair of Armani jeans, an Armani sweater and some Timberland boots. In other words, he was fine as hell.

After staring for a moment, he walked over and very abruptly said, "So, why did yo' girl try to skip you on the introductions?"

I took a few seconds to answer. "I guess she considers me off limits."

"Oh, are you?" he asked, after licking his thick lips.

I stared at his lips and imagined them on me for a minute. "It depends," I replied flirtatiously, toying with him.

"On what?" O.B asked.

"Umm ...a lot of things." I wanted to skip the subject so even though I knew it, I said, "Tell me your name again?"

"O.B!" he shouted over the music.

"That's unique."

"You think so?"

"Yes," I replied, sipping on the drink Sheba had just handed me.

"So, why does that tattoo on your face say QT?"

"That's personal," he responded.

"Oh," I said sarcastically. I didn't really give a fuck anyway.

"Does your friend always act like that?"

"Who?" I asked.

"That one," he said, pointing to Nicole.

With a sarcastic tone, I said, "Yeah, but it usually doesn't take her so long to make a scene. I guess she's losing her touch." I don't think he found my joke amusing because he turned around and walked away from me.

We made our way around the club to check everyone out. The place was pure heaven. Most of the guys were cute and dressed average but you could tell who the major players were from the jewels they wore around their necks. I never knew Richmond had it going on like that.

"Do these mothafuckas know how to party or what," Sheba said.

"Hell yeah," Nicole said in agreement.

DJ Lucky Lou put on Beyonce's 'Drunk in Love' and we all started screaming as we hurried to the dance floor. After Beyonce, the DJ put on some old school reggae. Sheba yelled, "Let's show these bitches how it's done!"

Now reggae was our shit, and we got down, right nasty when we danced to it. We were out on the dance floor winding our bodies to the sounds of Shabba Ranks when I looked up briefly and noticed one of the girls that Nicole was talking shit to outside in line, standing behind her. The girl was dancing but barely moving. Her eyes were fixed on Nicole. Nicole was so high and into the baller she was pressing her body up against, she didn't notice anything. I kept winding but slower as I scanned the dance floor. Several of the girls were positioned around us on the floor.

Being a former Marine taught me a lot of good shit. I could spot an enemy attack from a mile away before they could even get assembled and attack. But I wasn't by myself so I had to warn my girls without anyone suspecting anything. I danced in towards Brina.

"Bri, keep dancing but listen…some shit 'bout to go down. Them bitches from outside got us surrounded. I think it's 'bout seven or eight of them."

Brina breathed deeply. She tried to be calm but you could tell she was scared. She wasn't a fighter by any means but if you hit her she would defend herself. "Shit, Nicole always running her fuckin' mouth," Brina said.

"Yeah, I know. You tell Nicole what's up. I'ma get Sheba's attention."

"All right," Brina nervously squeaked out.

Just as I turned towards Sheba, out of the comer of my eye, I saw the girl behind Nicole push her in the back of her head. Nicole swung around with a vengeance. "Bitch, watch what the fuck ..."

The short fat girl cut Nicole's words mid stream as she swung and hit Nicole hard in the side of the face just to the left of her mouth.

"Naw, bitch, you watch what the fuck you doing," the girl yelled as she put on a show for her crew. Nicole, a bit dizzy, tried to swing back but before she could another girl had grabbed her from the back. Nicole's arms were locked in the girl's embrace while the short fat one combo'd on Nicole's face. The crowd on the floor dispersed. I ran towards the action but was tripped up by one of the crew. I jumped back up and noticed Brina running in the other direction as I jumped on the fat girl's back. I put my arm around her neck and choked her with all I had. One of the crew had apparently grabbed my hair and was pulling me back, but I didn't let go even though it felt like my hair was being detached from my scalp. I'm not sure if it was the same one or a different one that sent a fist crashing into my jaw. I still didn't let go of that fat heifer. I had no idea where Nicole had gone.

I heard one of the girls scream, "Bitch, let her go. She can't breathe. Let her fuckin' go."

"Fuck you," I screamed as I tightened my hold. I tasted the blood in my mouth. I didn't even realize that I had been hit in the mouth, which made me want to squeeze the life out of her even more. No one...I mean no one puts their hands on me.

The next thing I know, Brina, K-Dog and his crew were on the floor with security breaking everything up. The DJ stopped playing music. I was sort of in a daze as one of the security guards pried my arm from around that fat bitch's neck. I could hear DJ Lucky Lou admonishing us. "C'mon ladies, leave that mess outside. We're here to have a good time tonight."

Because K-Dog was cool with security, they let K-Dog, O.B, Quan and the rest of their crew walk us outside. I could hear the DJ starting the music back up as we got out the door.

"Where them bitches at? Fuck this shit, where them bitches at!" Nicole demanded.

Her face looked bad. Nicole wasn't used to losing a fight. But the appearance of her face said that we had lost this one.

"Security put them out the back door," Brina said. "C'mon let's go back to the car. We don't need no more drama tonight."

We all started heading back to the cars. Everyone began talking and laughing about the situation with the exception of O.B He walked behind us like a spoiled brat who couldn't have his way. And I think I was the only one who noticed it. Maybe they noticed it too, but just didn't care. This led me to wondering why I cared. If he didn't want to go out with us, he should've stayed home. All the pouting and frowning like a little bitch was unnecessary. I noticed he did it often.

When we reached my car, K-Dog suggested we go get a bite to eat at the Waffle House. I turned my nose up but since I was out voted I felt obliged to go against my better judgment. Once we reached Waffle House, we walked in and sat at a table that was big enough to seat us all. I didn't even bother looking at a menu. When the waitress came over I blurted out, "I'll take a coffee please!" I needed to wake the fuck up so I could drive us back to Norfolk. As far as I was concerned, tonight was a complete disaster and I wanted to take my butt home.

My girls just sat in silence because they knew once I got pissed that was it. They also didn't want to take the chance on getting left in Richmond because I was known for getting in my damn car and leaving a mothafucka.

With his face buried in his menu, O.B acted as though he didn't notice that his phone kept ringing.

15

"Yo son, answer yo' phone," Quan shouted, after rattling off at least five items he was going to order off the menu. No wonder he was kinda chunky. He was cute though...just not my type.

O.B shook his head.

"Let me guess, your girlfriend doesn't know you're hanging out tonight, does she?" I said sarcastically.

He gave me a look that let me know I hit a nerve.

"Mind yo' business!"

"Whatever," I said laughing. "Y'all niggas ain't shit."

Tired of his phone going off, O.B finally picked it up. When he saw who it was he fell back in his chair.

"Yo', who dat? The terminator?" Quan asked, laughing.

"Exactly," he said before answering it.

I was sitting two seats down from O.B and could hear the loud shouting. That's how bad she was cussing his ass out. They'd referenced her as the terminator. I wondered if she was his girlfriend.

"Damn, she mad as hell, ain't she?" Sheba said.

"You know just when we think we've gotten to the bottom of her craziness...there's another level," K-Dog said laughing.

He must've gotten tired of listening to her because he yelled, "I don't have time for this bullshit." Then he hung up the phone.

As everyone was ordering their food, K-Dog asked, "Zsaset, you don't want nothin' to eat?"

"No, I'm not hungry."

Brina shot him an evil eye. I guess she had her claws in him and didn't want him to consider the rest of us. Unfortunately for her, he seemed to like Brina as just a friend.

"K-Dog, Zsaset doesn't eat at places like this. She's used to fancy brunches with omelets and Mimosas," Nicole said, laughing.

"Oh you got jokes?" I asked pissed.

Nicole kept laughing which made me even angrier.

"Naw, I'm just saying you act like you're better than us sometimes. Like some eggs from a greasy spot is too good for you."

"Well, see that's where you're wrong?" Brina shouted across the table. "She don't even eat eggs."

The whole table broke out in laughter.

"Thank you," I said, rolling my eyes.

"I love you, Zsa!" Nicole said.

"Fuck you bitch," I replied, throwing my napkin at her.

While everyone else was enjoying their food, I sat stone faced ready to go. Sipping on my coffee as everyone else ate, I noticed to my right that some girls were arguing. They sound like me and my girls, I thought. I was in the middle of the waitress giving me a refill on my coffee when a plate flew pass me.

"Oh hell naw!" I yelled, as I ducked for cover.

Just that quick, a fight broke out in a restaurant. For some reason, all the girls went crazy and started attacking each other. The guys they were with were like WTF as they tried to stop them from beating each other. One of the men threw one of the girls to the ground to stop her. All I saw was ass and titties. Then another guy punched a girl in the face who was beating the shit out of his girl. He knocked her to the ground and then commenced to stomping her like she was a dude. That was it for me. I was out of there.

When I turned around, the rest of the crew was following me. My girls and I jumped in my car but before we could pull off, K-Dog suggested we stay in Richmond for the night.

"Y'all too fuck'd up to drive back to Norfolk."

Brina grinned widely from ear to ear.

"Plus, Sugar Ray here needs to hurry up and get some ice on that face." K-Dog pointed at Nicole. "Why don't y'all stay with us? I promise we'll behave like perfect gentlemen. You ladies can have the bedrooms and we'll sleep in the living room."

"Oh, hell no. I ain't giving my room up. Speak for yourself, man," O.B blurted out.

"Well, you have no choice if we decide to stay," I blasted.

"Who the fuck are you?"

"Who the fuck are you?" I yelled back. "We don't need your funky ass room. C'mon y'all, I can drive back."

"Boy, you ain't gonna kill me," Brina said.

We could all tell she really wanted to stay with K-Dog.

"Naw, I can't let you drive back like this. Don't worry, he'll give up his room," K-Dog insisted.

"Let's just stay here tonight. I'm tired," Sheba begged.

"All right, but keep him away from me, I don't like him. He has a serious attitude problem," I said, referring to O.B

"Deal. Y'all follow us," K-Dog said.

My instincts told me this wasn't a good idea but I went anyway. We had already been in a fight so I figured, what else could happen?

three...

We drove through the heart of Richmond at top speed. I had only driven maybe ten minutes when I felt my eyes starting to grow weary. Everyone else had fallen asleep giving me time to reflect on my life; I yearned for something, new and different. I wanted a new job, well more like a new career, more like my own shit. The more I thought, the sleepier I became. We ended up driving about fifteen miles outside of the city until finally we pulled into a neighborhood. The area where K-Dog and his friends lived was a quiet, resort-like, peaceful community, unlike the city where everyone looked like they'd steal from their own Grandma.

"Wake up, sleepy heads. We're here!" I yelled.

"Why you yellin', Boy? We hear you," Brina yawned.

"Well, then get the fuck up. I ain't taking nobody in the house tonight, so you better get up or you'll be sleeping out here with Big Foot.""Where the hell are we at?" Nicole mumbled through her swollen lips.

"We're in the suburbs of Richmond. Don't it look spooky? Ain't nothin' out here but trees. They don't even have street lights," I said as I looked around.

We gathered our belongings and followed the guys into the house. "Well, you ladies can make yourselves at home," K-Dog announced.

For the first time tonight, I realized K-Dog was about 6'5. He was taller than O.B and a whole hell of a lot nicer. Being the nosy person I am, I headed upstairs to case the joint. Something I picked up from watching way too much crime shows on television. A few minutes later, Nicole came up holding ice to her face. Now that everything had a chance to swell, she was looking like she was wearing a monster mask. I tried not to stare but I could barely see her pretty little face through the beep of swollen flesh. Her right eye was severely swollen and she had a huge bruise on her cheek. She got fucked up, I thought as I inspected her face.

"Zsaset, what you doing up here?" she asked.

"Hell, he told us to make ourselves at home. So that's what I'm doing. Besides, I wanted to make sure there weren't't any dead bodies up in here."

"Girl, it's not that big of a deal," Nicole said in disgust as I looked underneath the bed.

"Hell, we don't even know their real names. You know we're really crazy for doing this shit. If we get raped by these guys, all we can tell the police is a bunch of fucked up nick-names," I said.

"Shhh, I hear somethin' ,"Nicole said.

It was O.B's mean ass. "Is everything up to your standards, detective Zsaset?"

"Yes, everything is okay so far," I said, getting up from the floor. "What's your name again?" I faked.

"It's O.B"

"Where'd you get the nickname, O.B?"

"My friends. Why?"

"Nothing, just asking."

I laughed to myself thinking, how fitting, his friends named him after a tampon. It was probably because he acted like a woman on her period. O.B must have noticed the smirk on my face because he said, "Yeah, whatever."

O.B and Nicole went back downstairs. I checked the remaining rooms. Everything was cool so I went back downstairs only to find everyone asleep. I mean everyone. They were all lying on the floor over top of each other, especially Sheba and Quan who were sleeping way too close. They were so fucked up they couldn't even make it up the stairs. I wasn't sure about sleeping on the floor with a bunch of strangers, but I was too scared to sleep upstairs alone. So I squeezed in between the two couches and dozed off. That was the first time I had slept on a floor, and I was going to make sure it was the last.

I awoke the next morning in a panic. None of the guys were anywhere to be found. "What's wrong Zsaset?" Brina asked.

"I forgot to call Deonte and let him know I wasn't coming home last night."

"Oooooooh, he's gonna fuck you up. I thought you called him before you went to sleep."

"Well, you thought wrong," I said, rushing to dial Deonte's number.

"Bitch, don't get smart with me 'cause you gonna get your ass kicked."

I wasn't even worried about that happening. If he even thought about hitting me again, I would fuck his ass up. I may be a lot of things but a punk wasn't one of them. I would go round for round with anyone that put their hands on me, with the exception of my momma.

"What, Zsaset?" Deonte answered in a groggy voice. Shit, I was hoping it would go to voicemail.

"Hey. I forgot to call and let you know I wasn't coming home."

"Forgot, my ass. Where the hell are you?"

"I'm in Richmond."

"What the hell are you doing in Richmond?"

Deonte didn't hide the disgust in his voice.

"We went to a club and we were too dru... I mean too tired to drive back."

"So, Zsaset, tell me where you really are? I want details!"

I stumbled over my words but finally got it out, "We at the Days Inn in Richmond." I couldn't tell him we were staying with a bunch of dudes.

Deonte wasn't buying it. "Yeah, whatever." He paused for a moment. I prayed he was going to let it go but of course he didn't. "You know what Zsaset, you and your friends are some hoes. Zeta wants to talk to you."

Shit. Why did he have to put the baby on the phone?

"Mommy, you coming home now?"

Zeta's voice was so sweet. I was so irritated with Deonte for using her the way he did. I heard him in the background saying, "Ask her where she is Zeta?"

I put on my sweet mommy voice, "Hey Zeta, mommy will be there in a little while, Okay sweetie. I'll make sure to bring you something."

"Mommy, Barbie wants to talk to you." Shit. I wasn't in the mood for this.

"Ok baby, you and I will have a tea party with Barbie when I get home, but first put Daddy back on the phone."

A second later, Deonte got back on the phone.

"You're pathetic," he said. "I'm drawing up divorce papers. This shit is out of hand." He kept yelling as I held the receiver away from my ear. I gave him about a minute to vent before I hung up. I wasn't trying to hear that shit especially since he partied a lot, too. I was tired with a massive headache and this mothafucka wanted to yell. Oh, hell no.

After I hung up, my friends started cracking jokes. Everyone thought it was funny except me.

"If you were my wife, I would black both yo' eyes as soon as you walked in the house."

I turned to see who was talking and it was that smart-ass O.B I wanted to say, "Nigga, please," but I decided to take the more diplomatic approach. So, I replied, "Is that so? Well, if you were my husband and you gave me two black eyes you'd be walking around dick-less, fuckin' with me."

I usually didn't talk to people like that, but he pissed me

off. I guess I pissed him off too because he stormed up the stairs and slammed his door. Why did he feel like he had to say something anyway? This was between me and my husband. *He was not in the equation*, I thought to myself.

Since Deonte was already mad there was no need for me to rush home, so I fell back to sleep. I awoke later to the smell of pancakes and turkey bacon. My stomach was rumbling, so I followed the smell to the kitchen. K-Dog had his do-rag wrapped tightly on his head, engrossed in the preparation of breakfast. He was at the stove while everyone else played Spades at the table.

"What...you can cook? I'm impressed," I said to K-Dog. He smiled. I could tell he must've come from a good family or either he was the oldest sibling, because any other man would have just made himself breakfast.

I made myself a plate and took a seat at the table. When I was finished, I looked up from my plate and noticed O.B staring at me. He looked as if he wanted to cut my head off. So, I frowned back at him. Truly, I would have preferred to cut something else off of him. It was obvious he had a problem with me but at the same time it seemed to be his weird way of showing that he was digging me. He was sending mixed signals and it was driving me crazy.

"O.B, did you take care of that thang?" K-Dog asked.

"Naw, I'll go take care of it now," O.B answered.

He quickly ran upstairs to get dressed and when he came back down, he began pacing around the house like he was looking for something.

Quan got irritated and yelled, "What the hell you lookin' for, man?"

He kept fumbling around as if he didn't hear him. "I was lookin' for these, is that all right with you?" he barked, grabbing his keys.

"Ok, well you got them, now get the hell out."

Quan seemed really laid back. But I could tell O.B got on his nerves because they argued the whole time we were there.

23

I *Shoulda'* SEEN HIM *Coming*

Quan was called the Don of the crew. He looked half-black and half Chinese, obviously coming from a mixed couple. Sheba was on him hard and he seemed to be on her, too. I was willing to bet my next check they'd fucked at some point since we got to the house.

O.B seemed to be stalling. "You wanna go?" he finally asked looking at me.

I rolled my eyes as hard as I could. "Hell no, so you can kill me and leave me on the side of the road somewhere. I don't think so," I said.

"Ain't nobody gonna do nothin' to you, girl."

"Zsa, get your shit and ride with the man. You know you want to go," Sheba said.

She was right, I did want to go.

"Are you sure you want me to ride with you? I mean you've been pretty nasty to me."

"If I didn't want you to go, I wouldn't have asked."

I guess there were two sides to Mr. O.B cause his attitude towards me quickly changed. Last night, he hated my guts and now he wanted to go take a ride like we were friends.

When we got outside, my first thought was, I know he doesn't expect me to ride in this piece of shit.

"Come on, it's my ride around car."

"Geeezzz," I mumbled.

I slid in the car and looked over at O.B He glanced at me from head to toe and at that very moment, I was digging him. I was trying not to be obvious in checking him out. I couldn't help but notice how large his hands were as he gripped the steering wheel. Large hands often meant a big dick. Instantly, I got a little wet.

O.B was leaned way back in his seat. "Can you see where you're going?" I said seductively.

"I can see just fine, thank you," he snapped.

"Sorry. I just don't want to lose a limb 'cause you wanna take a nap in your seat."

O.B smiled. I guess he found my comment humorous.

24

His entire face lit up. His thick sexy lips spread neatly across his face. Everything about his face was dark and smooth except his enormous brown eyes. He had a scar to the left of his nose that gave his face a cute rugged look. I wondered what had happened to cause the scar but dared not ask him. At least not yet.

"You should smile more often, it looks good on you."

"You think so?" he asked, stroking his goatee. "Yeah, I do."

"So if I do, does that mean you won't be off limits to me?"

I smiled at him and buckled my seatbelt but I didn't say anything. The drive was crazy. It was like taking a field trip from The Jefferson's to Good Times. I couldn't believe all the buildings that were surrounded with police tape. Seeing all the crack-heads made me check my door, but nothing beats what I saw when we drove past a sign that read Mosby Court. It was a project on the east side of Richmond. There were apartment buildings with boarded up windows, men pissing outside in broad daylight, and used needles on the ground. This shit was unreal.

We parked on the main strip and O.B rolled down his window. A rotten-mouthed crack-head approached the car. The other smokers that stood on my side scared the wits out of me.

"What's up, O.B?" one of them yelled.

"What's up, Pipe?"

"These people are pathetic," I mumbled under my breath.

O.B told the crack-head to step back for a minute. He turned back to me. "What do you mean 'these people'? They're just like you and me."

I had obviously offended him which seemed to be easy to do, of course. What did he mean they were 'just like me'? The last time I checked, I was drug free. I frowned at O.B.

"Oh, I guess you grew up privileged, huh Zsaset?"

"Look O.B, I did grow up in the projects. But it didn't look anything like this. My family had pride and we tried harder to keep ourselves together because we knew people were already going to look down on us for living in government paid housing. These people look like they don't care about shit. We made it our business to get out of the projects as soon as we could."

"Well, some people don't have that choice," he said cutting the conversation short. He grabbed the keys from the ignition and opened the door.

"Maybe I used a poor choice of words when I said 'these people', but I was referring to the drug addicts, anyway. Now, where are you going?"

"I have to pick up something," he said. Before I could say another word, he slammed the car door. "Curiosity killed the cat," he said, as he walked away with a pipe-head named Gums.

I had suspected that K-Dog, O.B, Quan and the rest of their crew were drug dealers based on the way they lived. From the clothes they wore to the jewelry and furniture I'd seen in their home, I simply assumed something illegal was going on. This trip confirmed it for me.

Just great. Not only did he bring me to the projects, he left me in the car. I slumped down in my seat and began to observe the people outside the car. Crack-heads were searching the ground as if a magic self-generating crack rock was going to appear. The female crack-heads were dressed in dingy tattered short skirts and ripped nylons with lipstick smeared across their faces. They peered into cars that passed by looking for potential Johns. There were kids playing in the street without shoes. Where were their damn parents? I wanted to dig in my purse and give them money because they reminded me of the Somali kids I'd seen on PBS.

I always thought the place I grew up was bad. But compared to this place, it was Beverly Hills. *I am definitely blessed,* I thought to myself. I'll never take a nice home, healthy children and a refrigerator full of food for granted. It saddened me to see so much poverty. I mean, here I was looking down on people and I could easily be one of them. Zsaset never once thought about her own children. She was caught up in another world.

The sound of shattering glass interrupted my thoughts. I jumped and screamed at the same time. I turned to see that the back windshield of the car had been smashed out. A cinder block rested on the back seat. Without even knowing what I was doing, I jumped over to the driver's seat. My hand was trembling so bad I couldn't get the car started. Of course, I couldn't think straight enough to remember that O.B took the keys with him. I didn't even realize that the driver's side door was open until I heard the voice.

"Tell O.B he better leave my lil' brother alone. He might run these projects but he don't run my family!"

I couldn't tell you what this nigga looked like 'cause I didn't dare look at him. I could just feel him towering over me. I leaned my face forward on the steering wheel and didn't respond. I was too scared to say anything.

"You hear what the fuck I'm saying? Let that mufucka know that the next time it ain't gonna be his car…it's gonna be him."

When O.B returned a few minutes later, I was still in the same position with the door open. "Zsaset, what happened? You okay? What happened?"

I glanced at O.B and started yelling hysterically. "I don't know what just happened. You tell me! A nigga just smashed out your window and then started screaming at me about you and his lil' brother. I don't know what the fuck is going on!"

Something must have clicked for O.B "Oh, so those the games he wanna play? I'ma fuck that nigga up." He threw a large duffel bag in the car and told me to move over. He quickly jumped in, started the car and peeled out.

"How could you leave me set up like that? That was really fucked up, O.B," I shouted. He didn't respond. I positioned myself in my seat so that I was facing the opposite direction from O.B I gazed out of the window wondering how I always got hooked up with niggas like this.

O.B pulled over once we got in the suburbs. "Zsaset, I'm sorry about what happened over at Mosby Court. I swear nothing like that has ever happened to me over there. I wouldn't have left you there if I thought for one minute something like that was going to happen."

It was very interesting watching this side of O.B He was actually being sweet and he sounded sincere.

"It's cool. I guess there was no harm done," I said.

I thought I would take advantage of this opportunity to pry into some of O.B's business. "What's that in the bag?" I asked.

"There you go again with the questions. Can you please just sit back and shut up?" O.B's sweet demeanor was gone just as fast as it came.

"Don't tell me to shut up. My husband doesn't even tell me to shut up."

"That's because he's a punk."

"You don't know anything about my husband, so don't talk about him."

Pissed off, I twiddled my thumbs and tried to remain calm. It was one thing for me to put my husband down, but I'll be damned if he was going to.

After that, the remainder of the drive back was quiet and the tension between O.B and myself continued to grow. I decided to try to break the ice. "Do you have a girlfriend?" I asked.

"No, I don't. I have a wife."

"A wife," I said, flaring my nostrils. "Who the hell married your mean ass?"

"My wife," he said without expression.

"Do you have any kids?" I asked one too many questions.

"Yes, I have a son. Now stop asking me so many questions. I'm not going to tell you that shit again."

Here we go again, I thought. "Look, if you can't talk to me with respect, then don't talk to me at all." He must have known I meant business, so he apologized.

"So, you got kids?"

"Yes, I do," I said with a smile. "I have a daughter who's three and my son is six. I'm ready to get on the road so I can get back to them. It's only been one night but I miss them already."

"That's cool," he said, looking over at me.

O.B pulled up to the house and parked. I quickly grabbed O.B's arm when he proceeded to open the car door. I leaned over in my seat and looked him in the eyes. "You like me, don't you?"

O.B smiled. "There you go with the questions again."

I was extremely irritated by his response. "Nigga, please."

O.B put his index finger over my lips. "Yes, I do. Is that straight enough for you?"

"Yes, it is. So, where do we go from..." Before I could finish my sentence he pulled me closer and slipped his tongue damn near down my throat. His lips were soft and his kiss was fire. When O.B pulled back, I noticed the scar and tattoo on his face all over again. I wanted to ask about those initials once more, but instead said, "You kiss damn good to be so mean."

"Maybe I'm not mean. Maybe you just been pushing all the wrong buttons."

"Well, you got to show me the right buttons," I said as I got out the car, O.B followed.

"Well, that definitely can be worked out," O.B slowly said as he studied my body from head to toe. I got to the door first and rang the bell. O.B came up behind me very close as I stood at the door. He was so close that I felt the size of his dick rub against my ass. Between that boss move and feeling his breath on my ear, I was truly ready to give him some.

I turned just slightly. "Dag, nigga give me some space."

O.B backed up just a little. "Yeah, I'ma give you some space for now, Zsaset," O.B confidently whispered.

Brina, Sheba and Nicole all eyed me suspiciously when O.B and I walked in. I didn't realize it, but we had been gone for a while. "It's about to get dark so we better go," I said. "You guys ready, right?"

"We been ready!" Nicole said.

As we all stood in the driveway, I couldn't help but squirm in my jeans thinking about kissing O.B's juicy lips again. He ignited something in me that I lacked in my marriage. I didn't want everyone to know what was going on, so I sat in my car while they said their good-byes. Brina and K-Dog were leaning against K-Dog's car. I wasn't sure if anything sexual had happened with them, but knew something did with Quan and Sheba. They were the last ones to finally come out of the house, joined at the hip while Quan kept his hand stuck down the front of her pants. I smiled, happy for them all.

O.B finally walked over to me and asked if I was going to call him. I thought everyone was watching us, so I tried to act like I wasn't interested in what he was saying.

"All right O.B, work on being nicer to me the next time we talk," I whispered.

He smirked. "Yeah…O.K…Zsaset," he said as he walked back towards the house.

Damn, his body was cut, I thought to myself.

I didn't know it then but that was the beginning of something dangerous between O.B and I. I was about to take a ride with death and I didn't even know it.

four...

No one said anything about me and O.B for about the first thirty minutes of our drive home. I knew they were dying to know. Then out of the blue Nicole hit me in the back of my neck. The surprise attack made me swerve on the highway. My first instinct was to pull over and put the bitch out of my car, but I took a deep breath, counted to ten and told her not to do it again or she was going to regret it. I'd learned that shit in my mandatory anger management class I had been taking since I got kicked out of the Marines.

"Zsaset, since you ain't gonna bring it up on your own, what happened? Girl, give us the low down," Sheba smirked.

"What?" I asked playing dumb.

"Bitch, don't play, you know who I'm talkin' 'bout."

"Who, O.B?" I said, pretending to be baffled.

"Who, O.B?" Sheba imitated me in a cartoon-like voice. Everyone laughed.

"Oh, I mean nothing really," I said nonchalantly.

"Stop lying, Zsaset. Do you think anyone in this car is gonna tell Deonte? Stop trippin'. Tell us what happened?" Sheba urged, showing her impatience with my reluctance to talk.

Although we had been friends for years, I never told my girls every little thing I did. It was always in the back of my mind that if our friendship ended they would know all my busi-

ness and could use it against me later. So, I kept them and everyone else on a need to know basis.

I wasn't giving up any information, so they started as-
suming shit. "Y'all were looking kinda hot and heavy to me,"
Nicole said, determined to get all up in my business.

She was the one I knew the least amount of time, so I
definitely wasn't telling her. "That's 'cause you can't see too
well right now." I tried to make a joke and shift the conversation
to Nicole and the fight. It didn't work. Sheba and Nicole continued with their line of questioning. Brina was mostly quiet. I
think she thought that I would tell her everything once Nicole
and Sheba weren't't around. Brina and I were more like family
before we even met Nicole and Sheba. One night at a club,
Brina and I got into a fight with some girls who outnumbered
us. The attack came out of nowhere. We would've been killed if
Sheba and Nicole hadn't jumped in. The crazy thing was they
didn't even know of us but they had seen around from time to
time. From that day on, we've been thick as thieves.

Nicole smirked, "Y'all were gone quite a while today
and the look on your face when y'all walked back inside the
house said, guilty. And I know you not happy with Deonte."

"Who gave you permission to be in my business?" I
asked nastily.

"Don't get mad at me 'cause you cheatin' on your husband. Yo ass should've never said "I Do," in the first place. You
know you still got the hoe up in ya real thick."

"What? Where does she get this shit from?" I turned to
Brina and Sheba. There was a moment of silence until they all
burst out laughing. I silently reminded myself to watch that hoe.

• • •

After dropping everyone off, I thought of a plan for handling Deonte. I knew he was going to be pissed. He probably
has his bags packed again. He always did that when he got mad,
of course he never went anywhere. We would just fight and then

engage in nasty, amazing, make up sex as usual. In a weird sort of way I think Deonte was obsessed with transforming me into the perfect little housewife. I think he looked at it as some sort of competition or challenge that he didn't want to lose at.

Turning the doorknob slowly, I braced myself for Deonte's wrath, but he was cool and collected. What the hell is that all about? Why isn't he mad? I wasn't about to go looking for trouble, so instead I checked on the kids, took my clothes off and jumped in the shower. By the time I was finished, Deonte was sitting in the living room watching television. I cautiously sat on the couch next to him.

"Zsa, I just want to let you know you ain't doing nothing slick. I called the Days Inn in Richmond. They didn't have you, Brina, Nicole or Sheba as a guest there."

I played it off. "For your information, Deonte, the room was in Sheba's cousin's name. Damn, you always trying to check up on somebody." I pretended to be pissed by the fact that he doubted my word. "You need to work on that shit."

It was quiet for a moment but he kept watching me.

"Why'd you put the kids to bed so early?" I quickly tried to skip the subject.

"I fed them and put them to bed so I could have some me time," he said, flipping through the pages of the T.V. guide. "Someone had to feed them."

"What's that supposed to mean?"

"It means you weren't't here as usual, so I had to do it."

I knew Deonte wouldn't be able to maintain his calm demeanor much longer so I decided to go off before he did. I got up and walked to the kitchen to get a cup of water.

"Well, what about all the times I've had to do it. What, I don't deserve a break sometimes." I slung the cup of water on the floor. "I work and take care of the kids just like you do, probably more. So, don't give me that bullshit about somebody had to do it."

I stormed out of the room and went up to our room. I wasn't about to listen to his ass one more minute. I reminisced on the fact that when I was only five months pregnant with Zeta, Deonte was deployed to Japan for a year. I went through doctor's visits, pregnancy issues, and a complicated delivery all by myself until he came back a year later. I think the whole ordeal made me bitter towards him. I was home dealing with taking care of kids and paying bills while he was in Japan living it up. Now that he was home and actually had to be a father, he made it seem like he'd married the worst mother in the world. I wasn't about to take that title so he just needed to shut the fuck up and deal with it. I paced the floor pissed off that I had to come home and listen to Deonte's bull shit.

"Always acting like he my damn daddy instead of my husband! If it wasn't for these kids I would never come back to this place!" I said out loud.

I took a deep breath trying to calm my nerves, but it didn't work. Irritated, I slung the covers back, jumped into bed and snatched the remote off the night stand. I started flipping channels, but to my dismay, nothing was really on. A few seconds later, I heard my cell phone beep indicating that I had a text message. I reached over and grabbed my cell off the charger and opened the text from Brina:

Hey chic, you good over there?

I texted back with a smirk on my face:

Girl yes...he's in here getting on my last nerve but I'm not worried about Deonte's ass. He will be alright! What I am trying to do is...holla at that dude O.B LOL!

I smiled as I hit the send button

Brina texted me right back.

OMG Zsa! You off the hook! Just make sure Deonte don't murder your ass. You know y'all Marines crazy. Give him some of them goods and all will be forgiven. He will be up making break-fast singing in the morning! Good night!

I laughed out loud before texting back.

LMAO!! I know that's right!! Good night girl!

I put my phone back on the charger thinking about how much I enjoyed hanging out with my girls and acting like I was single. I wanted to get to know O.B really bad. At that point, I knew marriage wasn't for me. Exhausted, I decided to try and get some sleep. I was just about to doze off when I heard Deonte enter the bedroom. I played sleep, wondering why he wasn't sleeping on the couch like he usually did when he was mad at me. I opened one eye to peep his shorts and boxers hit the floor. I had to admit he was hung like a horse.

A few seconds later he slid into bed moving close up on me. "What the hell you think you doing?" I asked with an attitude. Truth be told, I was horny as hell but I had to make him suffer for his earlier comments.

"Come on, Zsa, I need you! I've been waiting for you all night. A nigga is backed up. The least you could do is please your husband!"

"Move Deonte, get off me!" I said, trying to push him away.

He wasn't taking no for an answer and just stared like he was determined to get some of me. Furious and tired, I ignored his attempts and turned my back on him. Not fazed at all by my reaction, he slid up behind me closer and started rubbing his twelve inches against my ass cheeks. Within seconds, it was rock hard. I was too exhausted to fight, or storm into the other room so I just laid there hoping he would rub on me, jack off and go to sleep.

However, that wasn't the case; he kept grinding and groping my ass. My body loosened when his touch started to arouse me. When Deonte realized that I wasn't rejecting him any longer, his grinding rhythm quickened. Soon, I felt my insides getting moist and my pussy tingling with sensation.

I closed my eyes and imagined I was in bed with O.B instead of my husband. Before long, I was moaning and groaning wanting him inside me. I reached back and grabbed his long dick. Deonte followed suit and separated my ass cheeks and slid inside me from behind. The excitement of feeling the wetness of my pussy drove him crazy. I tightened my inside muscle around his dick as he pounded harder and harder. I returned each thrust with more force, still thinking about O.B

"Oooooh, Zsa," I miss rubbing these big ass titties."

I said nothing. I didn't want him to know I was enjoying our little random fuck.

"Ahhhhh shit," he groaned, acting like he'd won a prize. "Who's pussy is this?" he asked, while quickening his pace.

His shit was feeling soooooooo damn good. Maybe if we just never talked to each other, but he served me with good dick a couple times a week, we could stay married?

I started slinging my plump ass back on his stone-like member. I could no longer hide the fact that his shit felt incredibly good. I grinded hard. My thrust quickened. My breathing intensified. I was fucking him just as hard as he was me.

"Say it's my pussy!" he shouted.

I tried to hold back the moans when I felt myself about to cum and a flow of juices running out my pussy. As my heavy breathing started to calm down, I felt Deonte's body quiver. He grabbed me tight and moaned "I love you, Zsa!" as hot sperm exploded inside me. He let out a loud sigh of gratification as he collapsed on the pillow.

"Yeah…yeah…yeah. Now get off me!" I yelled, turning over, pulling the covers over me and falling fast asleep.

five...

The next morning I dropped Ryan off at school early since his third grade class was going on a field trip. By the time I got Zeta to the babysitter's, I found myself late for work again. Sitting in the parking lot of the Marine Corp Exchange had quickly depressed me. Monday mornings were never good to me, but I pulled it together and quickly entered my job. I walked by my manager's office quickly in an effort to avoid talking to her, and more importantly allowing her to see that I was late again.

My direct boss was sixty-five years old and looked every day of it. She had worked at the Marine Corp Exchange for thirty years, and for at least fifteen years before she started working at the Exchange, she had worked every other job on the Norfolk Naval base. Everyone, including the Commanding Officer of the base wished her ass would retire. There wasn't one person on the base who liked her. I personally wanted to choke the shit out of her for some of the stunts she pulled. This woman was infamous for starting shit between the employees. She would make you feel comfortable, bait you into talking about one of your co-workers then go back and tell them. Treachery!

"Good morning, Zsaset," she said in her usual smart-ass tone.

Damn, she saw me. I doubled back and poked my head

in. "Good morning, Mrs. Bea."

"How was your weekend?" she asked.

"It was great," I said, imitating her wickedness. She didn't care how my weekend was. She was just trying to be funny with her phony ass.

I counted my drawer and before I could open my department, an elderly white lady stood in my line. I imagined myself telling her, "Get the fuck away. I ain't open yet, bitch," instead I said, "Give me a moment please, ma'am."

I had worked in the shoe department at the Exchange for about a year and half after being dishonorably discharged from the military. I didn't have any friends there. A few girls were phony with me, but I truly didn't like most of the workers, and they didn't like me either. But everyone knew my history, so they didn't bother me too much. Of course, there's always that one person who likes to push the envelope. Her name was Mindy and she worked in cosmetics. We were in orientation and training together when we were both new to the Exchange. Mindy was a skinny little white chick that looked like she threw up after every meal. The gossip around the store was she was taking medicine for depression and anxiety but it wasn't helping her.

On the third day of training I told her to shut up, after she kept asking stupid questions. Everyone was ready to go home at the end of each day's training session but she asked so many damn questions that they ended up keeping us there for an extra hour. The other people in the class and the trainer all appreciated me checking Mindy. Anyway, from that point on Mindy made it her business to get under my skin. Whenever I was on a break or away from my register, somehow Mrs. Bea always found out. I knew it was Mindy's ass. The Cosmetic's department was up on a platform and from her post, she could see me and my entire department. I would have long since whooped her ass if I could afford to lose my job.

As the day progressed, somehow I made it through. It didn't turn out too bad. I spent most of the morning fantasizing about O.B, and checking my watch every fifteen minutes or so. In between those intervals, I took unnecessary bathroom breaks driving my co-workers crazy. At lunch time, I waltzed into the cafeteria only to see Mindy's face grinning my way. She was seated with two other girls that worked in Cosmetics. I got my food and sat at the only open table which happened to be right behind Mindy's table. She kept giving me dirty looks as she talked shit about me loud enough, purposely, so that I could hear her.

"What's her name, Zsashit?" The other girls cracked up. "No seriously, that's not it? Oh my God, I was getting ready to invite her to eat with us. I was going to say, Zsashit, come join us."

Mindy and the other two were almost hysterical.

"Oh my God, and you mean that's not her fucking name. What's her fucking name? Damn, her mother should have given her a normal name. Maybe that's why she always has an attitude, 'cause her name is all fucked up. Damn, she probably just wants to be called Mary or Jane or some shit like that."

Mindy and her friends were in tears now.

I tried to ignore her but it became clear that I wasn't going to be able to. I tried one of my anger management techniques but she kept running her mouth. So, I slowly stood. I walked over to her. At that moment, I didn't care about the consequences. Mindy's eyes got big when I bent down and put my face in hers. Her friends instantly stopped laughing. I took my hand and smashed her in the face. I knew her skinny ass wouldn't do anything back so I wasn't too worried about a fight breaking out. When her head snapped back and we were face to face again I said, "Honey, you don't know me...like you think you do. So stop running your fuckin' mouth before I beat your ass like you stole something from me."

I waited for her to say something back, but she didn't at first. I mean, I prayed she said something because I wanted a reason to tax that ass just one good time.

Feeling my job was done, I cleared my table. As I

walked slowly towards the door, I gave each and every one of
them eye contact. My eyes said, "Say something and watch you
get beat down." As I walked out the door I heard Mindy say,
"You'll be sorry you did that, Zsaset."

"Whatever bitch!" I yelled back.

I should've waited until we got off of work to confront
Mindy, but I just had to say something to her right then and
there. I had to let her and those other bitches know I was not to
be fucked with.

It was nearly 2:20 and I only had ten minutes left on my
lunch break. That's when O.B popped in my head. I wondered
what he might be doing so I gave him a call. The phone rang
several times before someone answered.

"Hi. Is O.B home?" I asked. I didn't recognize the voice.
It wasn't Quan or K-Dog.

"Naw," the voice on the other end replied.

"Okay, could you tell him Zsaset called?"

"Maybe. If he ever comes back, I'll tell him. We can't
find him."

"Can't find him?" I asked. I started damn near hyperven-
tilating. I thought about that crazy guy from Mosby Court. What
if he'd made good on his promise to hurt O.B? When was the
last time you saw him?" I spat.

The person didn't respond so I looked at my phone. To
my astonishment the guy had hung up on me. What the hell did
he mean 'If'? His statement bothered me for the rest of the day.
I even gave back the wrong change to customers a few times because I couldn't stop thinking about O.B I'd texted Brina asking
her to call K-Dog for info, but hadn't gotten a response yet.

As if my day couldn't get any worse, Mrs. Bea came
near my register and told me I'd better watch myself. She re-
vealed that my case worker, Mrs. Smith had called, asking for
an updated report on me. I immediately spazzed out, wondering
if a family social worker calling my job was legal. The situation
immediately sent my mind back in time. One day back in the
summer I was cooking spaghetti and meatballs for dinner. De-

onte and I got into an argument about a VIP pass he found in my purse. A guy at the club had given it to me the weekend before.

"Who did you have to fuck to get a VIP pass?" Deonte scoffed.

"Deonte, I told you before, don't go in my damn purse!"

"I didn't touch your purse. Zeta went in your purse," Deonte yelled.

"Yeah whatever, Deonte. You're always snooping and looking for something. You act like such a little bitch. I don't go through your shit. Remember punk, I'm supposed to be the bitch in this relationship!"

Deonte became enraged. He glared at me with his fist clenched. He drew back his right fist and punched a hole in the dining room wall. His fist went clear through to the other side of the wall.

"Zsaset, you gonna fuckin' learn how to talk to me with respect. You ain't gonna keep disrespecting me!"

Deonte and I continued to yell obscenities back and forth at one another. Meanwhile, Ryan came over to attempt to mediate just as he always did. Ryan put his hand on Deonte's side to get his attention. Deonte paid Ryan no mind. He didn't realize he was standing to his side. In a rage, Deonte grabbed his baseball bat to use as a scare tactic for me. The moment he swung back, he ended up striking Ryan forcefully in the chest.

The blow knocked Ryan out. He fell to the floor and I franticly yelled, "Call 911, call 911, Deonte!"

Deonte wouldn't budge. He was still in a blind rage. He even pulled the phone cords out of the wall. Has this mothafucka lost his mind? I looked around the house for something to throw at his ass, but I had to take care of my child first. I ran to the patio door and yelled across the street for my neighbor, Karla to call the police. Meanwhile, Ryan laid in my arms as I rocked him in the middle of the kitchen floor waiting for the paramedics to arrive. It seemed like it took them forever.

By the time the paramedics arrived, Deonte was on the couch like nothing happened. On the way to Bayside Memorial

Hospital I thought to myself, *if something is wrong with my baby I'm gonna kill Deonte's ass.* If his real father was any good, he'd kill his ass, too.

The doctor examined Ryan and ran some tests. After a few hours they said he would be fine. He went on to tell me that a social worker was on her way to speak with me.

"Talk to me about what?" I remembered asking.

"Well, ma'am when I asked your son what happened, he told me your husband hit him."

"Yeah, that's right. We were arguing."

"I know, ma'am. When there is a case of suspected child abuse, I am required by law to inform Child Protective Services," the doctor said in a solemn tone.

"Child abuse," I said in a state of shock.

What if they tried to take Ryan from me and place him in a foster home? What am I going to do? I paced for about an hour before a tall, extra- dark woman in a gray Limited pants suit appeared. "Good afternoon, are you Mrs. Jones?" she said, extending her hand.

"Yes."

"I'm Mrs. Smith from Child ..."

"I already know who you are," I said, cutting her short. I hated the way she peered over her thin wire glasses. And especially hated her mushroom styled wig.

She explained to me the procedure and that she had to talk to Ryan before her final decision was made. She left me standing in the hallway. I was mad as hell at Deonte's ass.

The look on the social worker's face when she walked out of Ryan's room scared me. She informed me that based on what he told her, it was her decision to put him in the care of someone else.

I nearly fainted.

I had given birth to a child that the state wanted to take away from me.

"Someone else, like who? Where will he stay?" I panted.

"Mrs. Jones, we have foster parents who are ready to

provide care and shelter to children who need it."

I started to cry. "Pleaseeee, is there anything else we can do? Please. My son only has me. He doesn't have his biological father in his life. Pleaseeeeeeee, don't do this," I begged with tears flowing like The Nile. I dropped to my knees in front of everyone.

"The only thing I can tell you is that if you have a relative that Ryan can stay with, we will talk to them and visit the home to see if it's safe for Ryan. If we determine that the home is safe for Ryan, then he would be able to stay with that relative until Child Protective Services determines that your home is suitable for Ryan to return."

I swear I didn't want to, but I called my mother. I knew she would agree to keep him. Ryan was without a doubt her favorite grandchild. Before long, my mother showed up, passed all the requirements with flying colors, and saved Ryan from going into foster care. Of course it wasn't long before we broke Child Protective Services' rules. Ryan ended up spending half his time with us and half his time with my mother. To date, that order hadn't changed, and apparently Mrs. Smith's bamma ass is still watching.

I Shoulda' SEEN HIM Coming

six...

Strangely, I decided to stay in and relax the next Saturday night. After dinner, I flopped on the couch and opened a Heineken. The phone rang. I grabbed it, figuring it was Brina or Sheba. I was prepared to tell them I wasn't going out.

"Oh, hey, Ma."

I was surprised to hear my mother's voice this late on a Saturday night. My mother went to church at the crack of dawn every Sunday. It didn't matter if she'd come down with the flu, or had diarrhea running down her butt cheeks; she never missed a service.

"You busy, Zsa? Where the kids?" I sensed uneasiness in my mother's voice.

"No, the kids are asleep. What's going on, Ma? Is something wrong? You need something?"

My mother hesitated, "Oh, well, ah, kinda."

"Ma, just spit it out." I hated when she beat around the bush. "All right, Zsa. Is ah, is Deonte there?"

"Yeah, he's sleep though. Why, is this about him?"

"Yeah, Zsa. It's about Deonte."

I was quiet and so was she for several seconds. If she didn't say another word at that moment, I knew what she was about to tell me. Ma's voice cracked, "I've been trying to get up the nerve to tell you for the last three days, Zsa."

I didn't say anything. It's not like I didn't see the signs a long time ago, but I didn't take heed to them—coming in the house late claiming he was out with his friends, concerned about his appearance all the time, and never having any extra money for me. That fool thought he was really doing something.

My mother went on to tell me that while visiting her best friend Ida, she noticed Deonte's car parked out front.

"Zsa, I made sure to walk close to the car to make sure it was his." She then paused as if she couldn't finish. "I...I...I just about fainted when I saw him and another woman walking to his car. I wanted to believe it wasn't what I thought, but Deonte wrapped his hand around her waist. And..."

"Say no more, Ma," I told her.

"I didn't want to hurt you, baby. That's why I waited so many days. I haven't even been able to sleep."

"I know, Ma. Don't you worry about me. I got this."

"And Ida said his car is over there a lot. That bastard," she blasted. "He needs Jesus."

Mom and I talked for a while longer. I told her why I actually married Deonte so quickly. It was my fictitious fairytale of gaining some stability in my life. I didn't want to seem like a failure to my family. My older brother, Frankie always did everything perfect. He was happily married to little miss perfect, had three little perfect kids, and lived in the perfect little house, in the perfect little neighborhood. They got on my nerves and I often avoided family functions so I wouldn't have to see them. So, of course, when Deonte proposed, I jumped on the opportunity to make my family proud. Our honeymoon phase lasted about three weeks, before we were at each other's throats. Anyway, for a long time, Deonte and I pretended to be the Brady Bunch in the presence of my family. However, it wasn't long before we were found out.

Sort of like my mom's story with my dad, bullshit. Just like my mom, I was looking for any man to be my father. I started to find solace in the world, the dark underbelly of the streets. I quickly learned that the problems I was having were from an underlying issue-my need for male attention.

I never knew my father but I often wondered if my family life would have been different had he been around. My mother raised me the best way she knew how. It was impossible for her to play both mother and father, but damn if she didn't try. But her working two jobs only left me to raise myself. The streets became my parents. And guess what my new parents gave me? A big belly at fifteen.

Looking for love in all the wrong places, I slept with any and everyone, leading to my early pregnancy and depression diagnosis.

My mother never really spoke ill of my father, but she was never short on stories about him. One story that always stood out in my mind was the story she told me about how she had to sneak money from him just to get pampers and milk. Although the story was comical, it often angered me. What kind of man fathers a child and then refuses to take care of it?

Being a father is more than just sending a check to your baby's momma. It's giving that child love and teaching them to have confidence and high self-esteem. All the things I lacked. I subconsciously looked for the love and nurturing I didn't get from my father in my intimate relationships. No wonder none of my relationships worked and I sucked at parenting. My standards were set too low. Who could blame me? I didn't have anyone around to show me how a real man loves and cares for a woman.

After hanging up from my mother, I filled up a large pitcher with ice cubes and extra frigid cold water. I went into the bedroom where Deonte was sleeping and poured the entire pitcher on him. Deonte jumped up screaming.

"What the fuck, Zsaset?"

"This is just the beginning, mothafucka." Deonte's angry expression turned to one of shock. "Nigga, I know you ain't think you was slick. All dirty laundry comes out eventually, baby!"

"What are you talking about?"

"You and one of your bitches was spotted!"

His expression changed. Deonte stood shivering saying, "Let's talk about this."

"Nigga, there's nothing to talk about. I know who she is," I lied with a straight face.

His next set of words threw me for a loop. "Ah, shit, Zsaset. I'm so sorry. I know our marriage is rocky, but I never meant to fall for somebody you know."

My eyes shot to the back of my head. Quickly, I contemplated my next move. It was detective time.

• • •

Over the next week, we walked around the house like we were strangers. The nights were even worse because we both refused to sleep on the couch. I despised Deonte. All I could think about were the lies he'd told and him making love to a bitch who knew me. Several nights I woke up wanting to kill him in his sleep. I tried to keep it together, but it got harder every day. We talked about one of us moving out. Deonte reminded me that neither of us could afford to. I hated to admit it, but he was right. So we decided we would both stay at the apartment, until he could afford to take care of himself and pay me child support. Basically, we agreed that our relationship was over.

I was so excited when I finally got a call from O.B asking me to visit him. I was so glad to hear his voice considering Brina could never find out anything about his whereabouts.

"Zsaset, what's up girl?"

"O.B?" I said.

"Yeah…what's up?"

"Nothing. It took you long enough to call me."

"My fault. Shit's been hectic, but I been thinkin' 'bout you though."

"I can't tell," I said seductively.

"When am I gonna see you again?" O.B cut to the chase.

"How 'bout this weekend?"

"Sounds good,"

I didn't want Deonte to walk in on me so I told him I needed to go. I felt heat rush through my body as I hung up the receiver. I wasn't sure what I was doing with O.B, but I knew I needed to see him again. This man turned me on in a way I never imagined. I definitely had a weakness for evasive men with a rough exterior. The problem was O.B was married and so was I, for now. I had no idea what the situation was with O.B's marriage. I had to consider the fact that maybe he was happily married and just wanted me as a side chick. I figured I would work hard on getting him to tell me about his situation the next time I saw him.

I made the necessary arrangements and asked my mother to watch Zeta and Ryan. She questioned me about my trip, but of course I didn't tell her anything. How could I tell her I was going to see another man? And no matter how crazy my marriage was, I was still married. I could hear my mother, the devout Christian, preaching, "Thou shalt not commit adultery." I knew she was right, but I was tired of being miserable, undersexed, and under-satisfied. Not even God could get me out of this. I wanted a real relationship and I was hoping O.B was the man who could give it to me.

• • •

Before I left for Richmond that Friday evening, I called O.B. The anticipation of being with him made me pause briefly and take a deep breath. After the fourth ring, he answered.

"Hi," I said, trying to sound as sexy as possible. "I'm on my way and I just wanted to make sure you're gonna be there when I get there."

"No doubt, baby," he said, making me wet between my thighs.

"All right, I should be there around eight o'clock. Have my bubble bath ready."

"Oh, so that's how you feeling? I'll see you when you get here, sexy," he said.

I must have arrived in record time. Hearing O.B's sexy voice made me do 90 mph all the way to Richmond. With my MCM purse thrown across my shoulders, I walked into the bachelor's pad with a humongous grin on my face. O.B strolled over to me and grabbed my bags. I spoke to Quan as I followed O.B up to his room. I almost stepped on his five rows of sneakers that took up most of the floor. I sat on the bed and before I knew it, he was on top of me giving me CPR. O.B must have sensed my hesitation. He lifted off of me and glared into my eyes.

"I missed you, girl."

"Oh, did you, now?"

"Yeah, Big Booty, I did."

As we lay across his bed, we talked and got to know each other a little. I was amazed to find out we had so many things in common. We both liked karate flicks and were exceptional bowlers. More importantly, we both wanted to be entrepreneurs; legal ones. I shared with him my dream of owning my own clothing store, and how I wanted to eventually franchise my company.

O.B talked about wanting to buy his mother a house in North Carolina so she could be near her family. He said he simply wanted to convert all his money into a legal, legitimate business. He liked carpentry work so flipping houses was an option. The money wasn't so much for himself, but for his family. He also wanted to have a college fund set up for his thirteen year old son so he wouldn't have to work while getting his degree. His dreams paralleled mine, although I didn't really speak on it. Sometimes the pain of not having Ryan with me consumed me so much that it just seemed easier to ignore the situation.

After relaxing a little more, O.B popped a bottle of

champagne. He looked at me with those sexy eyes, and I felt my panties moisten within seconds. I tried not to show my eagerness, because I wanted him to work for good pussy. I needed him to lick me up and down and to feel his tongue flick across my clit a few times before I let him get all up in it. I tried to excuse myself to go to the bathroom.

"Remember my bubble bath?" I reminded him, trying to sound real sexy.

In a split second, his demeanor turned commanding, making it clear that he was in charge…not me.

"Later," he said, while kissing me hungrily and pushing me back down on the bed.

As soon as I felt the size and hardness of his dick, I couldn't even fake. My body temperature shot up and I wanted him bad. I tugged on his zipper so I could get my hands on that thing. He grinned at me and slipped off his pants. Damn, his dick was pretty! I pulled off my jeans, exposing my red lace thong. I could tell he liked what he saw from the slight grin that was on his face. He slid my thong down my thighs with his teeth. Then he slowly licked me from my ankles all the way back up to my inner thighs, while gently massaging on my D cups. He teased the shit out of me, letting his tongue dance all over my booty before plunging it deep inside my middle. That was it for me; I was in love with this pussy-eating mother fucker.

"Fuck me now, O.B.," I moaned over and over again, getting louder each time. I held on to his head tightly. Purring like a kitty, my hips rose mid-air and I came harder than I ever thought I could.

"Oh, I see this is a first come, first serve basis," he said, showing no signs of being threw with my ass.

Before I knew it, he flipped me over on my stomach to go in for the kill. He put his tip in and stopped. I turned around and looked at him over my shoulder like he was crazy. "Beg for it," he commanded. I did just that. I lost my breath when he pushed all ten inches of it inside me.

In.
Out.
In.
Out.
Faster.
Faster.

His jewels made a slapping sound hitting against my ass. It was just as long as Deonte's, but thicker. Way thicker, juicer…and better. O.B's stamina was off the hook. Although I had already come again, I tried to keep up, but he just kept going and going, like the Energizer Bunny. If it had been the Olympics, he would definitely have won the gold for the Shot Put. I knew my shit was going to be sore for days, but I loved every minute of that good pain. It had been way too long since I had felt that good. His sex reminded me of some BBD lyrics: "Slap it up, flip it, rub it down, oh nooo, this dick is POISON …" And I was ready to die for it.

Finally, he reached his climax when we heard a knock at the door.

"Who is it?" O.B yelled, pulling out. "It's me, Quan. It's time to go, man."

"Time to go where?" I asked.

"Oh shit, I forgot. I have to go take care of some business."

"Business, uh?" I said with a smirk. O.B shot me a quick glance.

"Yeah, it's nothing. Look there's a mall near here. He dug in his pockets and threw a wad of money on the bed.

"Why don't you go do some shopping? By the time you finish, I'll be back," he said walking out the room.

I was so pissed off, I couldn't think straight. Who does he think I am? A trick or something, I thought to myself. After I counted the money, I didn't care what he thought I was. There was roughly twelve hundred dollars in my hand. If tricks got paid like this, then I'd be his trick for the day. So, off to the mall I went.

My first stop was to Nordstrom. Browsing through the store I noticed the new Diane von Furstenberg. I grabbed a handful of outfits and strutted towards the dressing room. The wrap dress fit me like a glove. But the rest looked equally as good. I couldn't decide so I bought them all. I wasn't usually this frivolous with money but since it wasn't mine I decided to have fun.

After spending almost every dime he gave me, I headed back to the house. I walked into the room to find O.B on the phone. Anxious to show him what I bought, I emptied the bag of clothes on the bed. I could tell something serious was going on by the way he hit his fist on the bed. O.B began yelling loudly. I couldn't tell what it was about but it was clear he wasn't happy. I stood there being nosy. Trying to divert my attention, he asked what I bought.

"Something I think you'll love to take off me later," I said, holding my slinky bed time special.

"Umm, I can't wait. Let me just finish up with my man then I'll get up witcha."

"Okay." I kissed him on his cheek.

I unraveled myself from his arms, and went to prepare for round two. I took my bubble bath and pampered myself for a while. When I came out of the tub, O.B was no longer in the bedroom. Once I was in my Victoria's Secret sheer, Barbie doll teddy, I yelled for O.B He walked in the room speechless.

"So, what do you think of the color red?"

"It just became my favorite color," he said, licking his lips. Needless to say, that time around was better than the first.

● ● ●

On my last night in Richmond, O.B took me to see Denzel's latest movie, and then to some new, fancy restaurant at Short Pump Mall. We talked for hours about our plans for the future. He talked a lot about wanting a different life for himself. He said he'd gotten himself into a very dangerous situation. That kinda talk sent chills through my body. I wanted to know more so I started in with tons of questions.

"So, am I in danger by being with you?"

"Hell no, I'll kill a nigga if they even come near you."

I smiled. Feeling protected was a good thing. It was something I wanted for my kids, too.

"You ever killed anybody?"

He laughed. "Next question…"

"Ever been to jail?"

"Many times," he responded quickly.

"Ever been gay?"

"Hell no!"

"I'm just making sure."

I was enjoying myself, but in the back of mind I wondered about O.B's wife.

"So, what's the deal with you and your wife?"

"She does her thing and I do my mine," he said, sipping on his Cranberry and Ciroc.

"How long has it been that way?" I asked digging deeper.

"About two years."

"Oh."

"She doesn't live here, Zsaset."

"That's weird."

"Yeah, but our arrangement is different. Besides, we're getting divorced.

"That's what they all say," I countered.

His energy level went all the way down. "It's real complicated. But it's not working out. We fight all the time and it is starting to affect my son, so we're just gonna call it quits."

"Oh," I stated then asked the waiter for another cocktail.

"What about you?" he asked.

"Ditto," I said.

O.B laughed.

"What you mean?" O.B said with a confused smile.

"I mean we're getting divorced, too ... we got married after I got pregnant ... it's not working out ... we're fighting in front of the children, etc. etc."

We both cracked up at the irony of how similar our situations were. We talked a little more and then we interrupted by his phone ringing. It was his wife and he didn't want to answer but I told him it was okay, so he took the call.

While they talked I continued sipping on my drink. Their conversation was bizarre, nothing like a normal husband and wife. And there was lots of talk about money and do's and don'ts. Then the unthinkable happened. He told the bitch he loved her and blew her a damn kiss before hanging up.

O.B knew I was upset but he assured me that he was just trying to keep the peace until he filed for divorce. He assured me we'd spend more time together real soon, but that he had business to take care of, and I needed to get back to Norfolk before it got too late. I started to end things before they even got started but I was still having sex with Deonte so I was doing the same thing; lying for a living

Danette Majette

seven...

I spent the next weekend and almost every weekend after that with O.B in Richmond. Summer time was quickly approaching, and I was having the time of my life. One Sunday, all hell broke loose when I returned home. Deonte and I got into our biggest fight ever. But this time it was even more physical.

When I walked in the house that Sunday I could tell something wasn't right. Shit was all over the floor. I slowly walked in and stopped in the middle of the living room trying to take inventory. For a moment it looked as if someone had broken in, but I quickly noticed that both the television and stereo were still there. Deonte walked from the back bedroom in a pair of boxers, wearing a hat and gloves. He looked as if he had been crying. Out of the blue, he threw something at me that turned out to be a picture.

Deonte had found a selfie that O.B and I had taken hugged up together in his car. I don't think Deonte would have been so angry except for the fact that Zeta was in the picture asleep. It was a night when O.B and I had met at a strip mall half way between Richmond and Norfolk just to see each other and talk for a while. I didn't have a babysitter so I bathed Zeta, put her in her pajamas and after she fell asleep, put her in the car. She didn't wake up until the next morning in her bed. She never knew she had been out of the house. Anyway, Deonte didn't know any of these details. He was rabid with anger.

"Bitch, how you gone have my baby girl around some bitch ass nigga just 'cause you fuckin' him?"

I wanted to cuss Deonte out but something inside me told me not to. I wasn't sure where his gun was. He seemed almost deranged with anger so I attempted to reason with him. "Deonte, it ain't what you think."

These were apparently the wrong words to say to him because he lost any remaining composure he had.

"What the fuck you mean, it ain't what I think?" He pulled the picture up on Instagram, shoved it in my face and yelled, "Zsa, look at the fuckin' picture. Pictures don't lie; it is exactly what I think."

"Look, calm down!"

Deonte pushed my head back. I fell back and tripped over my purse. I fell to the floor and hit the lower part of my back on the side of the couch. I jumped up in spite of the pain. Deonte started swinging and even though he stood a foot over me, his hits didn't faze me. I started swinging on his ass. He threw me down on the floor a couple times, but I kept getting up. The last time he knocked me down I came back up swinging so hard, I left my mark on him. With a piece of broken glass I put a two-inch gash in his chest. He looked down at the cut in shock then looked back at me.

"Yeah, that's right. Hit me again, bitch. The next time it's gonna be your throat that gets slashed," I said.

I was just about to pounce on his ass again when I heard Zeta cry out, "Daddy. Daddy."

I was so mad at him for hitting me I didn't even think what a scene like that would do to her. After calming her down, I assured her that he was all right. He thought I was just going to roll over and cry. He had it all wrong. That shit was not happening. I was not about to let him put his hands on me. It was either him or me.

• • •

The next morning, I called O.B and told him what happened the night before. He immediately went into a frenzy.

"Pack yo' shit and just leave him," he said.

"And just where am I supposed to go?"

"Move up here with me."

"How am I gonna do that? You're married, remember?"

"She doesn't live in Richmond, remember?" he shot back.

"What about my kids?"

"What about them? Bring them with you. We have enough room."

"I don't know. I have to think about it."

"What is there to think about? Do you want to stay with a man who hits you?"

"That's a low blow," I told him.

"I call it the way I see it."

After that conversation I called Brina to see what she thought. She hadn't been too happy with the fact that I hadn't been asking her to ride with me to Richmond every weekend. I truly wanted to, but O.B and K-Dog forbade me. It seemed that K-Dog wasn't interested in Brina anymore. He said she just wasn't marriage material, and at thirty-nine his criteria in women had changed. I still loved Brina, and was thankful for her good advice about the move.

It took me two days to make up my mind. Even though, I knew I would miss my friends and family, I agreed to go. Usually, decisions like this took a lot of planning. But I figured what the hell; things couldn't get any worse than they already were.

My mother was the first on my list to call about the decision. We had the kind of relationship that my girlfriends only dreamed of having with their mothers. We were like two peas in a pod. So I knew this sudden move was going to be very upsetting for her. But nevertheless, I told her that I was leaving De-onte and moving to Richmond. It didn't surprise me that she supported my decision even though she knew it was a mistake.

"Zsaset, I'm not so sure about this," she said. "I'm gonna support you in whatever you do, but just think on it real hard first. I wish you would just move in with me. "

"Ma, I know how you feel, but I need to leave here. I've always wanted my own clothing store and I think Richmond would be a good place for me to open it. Besides, I need a fresh start."

My mom was silent for a few seconds. "Well why don't you stay here and open it? I'll even take some money out of my retirement to help you."

My heart melted. I appreciated my mother's offer but this was something I needed to do on my own and I wasn't going to stop until I made her proud.

"I can't tell you what to do, but I don't think you should take both of the kids. You're gonna be in a new city and it's gonna take time to settle down. You can't do that with both of them kids. Let Ryan stay here with me."

Her facial expression reminded me that her worry about Ryan was deeper than taking him to a new city.

"You're worried about Mrs. Smith, aren't you?"

She shook her head.

"That woman made it clear that if another incident came across her desk she'd take him away forever." The lines in her face crinkled even more. "Forever, Zsaset," she repeated sternly. I think for now we should play by the rules. Why don't you go there and get settled then apply to get him fully back in your custody."

I didn't like what my mother was saying, but she made a lot of sense, so I accepted her offer.

"Okay, Ma. I'll leave Ryan with you. But Zeta's going with me."

She huffed before asking, "Where y'all gonna live?"

"I have some friends who live there. They said I could

stay with them for a while at least until I get a job and find a place of my own."

In an uneasy tone she said, "Well, that's nice of them."

My mother was no dummy. She knew me really well.

"I'm just gonna put my trust in God that you'll be okay up there," she said.

Now that I had my mother's blessing, I started packing my things. I was excited and scared at the same time. What if things didn't work out the way I thought they would? After all, I had only known O.B for a short period of time. That seemed to be a growing trend with the way I jumped into relationships. But I came to the conclusion that I had to stop dwelling on the negative and try to think of it as a new beginning.

Later that night, I called Sheba and filled her in. She knew that O.B and I had been hanging out but she was shocked when I told her that Zeta and I were moving in with him and the other guys.

"Zsa, you sure that is a good idea. O.B is like a Dr. Jekyll and Mr. Hyde. He's a fuckin' maniac. One minute, he's all nice and the next minute he's tripping on your ass."

"Sheba, O.B has been nothing but nice to me for a good while now. Sure, we got off to a rocky start but he's actually a nice guy."

"I don't know, Zsa, you sure you know what you're doing?"

"No, I don't. But I'm sure I can't stay with Deonte any longer. One of us gon' end up dead."

"Yeah…I feel you on that 'cause that nigga's crazy. I hear them stories about them Marine niggas gong off the deep end and killing everybody in their damn house."

Her words freaked me the hell out. "Look, I got to get packed, I'm gonna call you later on."

"All right, girl. But just let me go on record that I think you're making a huge mistake. I'm not saying you have to stay with him but don't leave town where you're close to your family and friends. What if you get to Richmond and O.B turns out to be another Deonte?"

Who knew she would be right?

eight...

By the time Deonte got home, most of my things were packed. I had two big suitcases sprawled across the bed. He looked like he'd seen a ghost. I don't know why. Did he really think I was going to stay with him after last week? He could be so bipolar sometimes. One minute he'd call me out of my name and then in the next minute he wanted some ass. I was over it!

"Where are you going?" he snapped.

"Take a wild guess, Einstein," I said in a taunting voice.

"Are you going to your mother's house?"

"No, I'm moving to Richmond...leaving your ass."

"So, you just gonna pack up and take my daughter to Richmond?"

"Ummm, let me see...Yeah," I said, continuing to throw my clothes in my suitcases.

"Zsaset, Zeta is only three years old. Why would you do that to her? Why would you uproot her from her family and friends?"

"You can get her on the weekends and she'll make new friends? Like you said, she's only three. She'll adjust!"

"Fuck this shit. You can take your son, but Zeta is staying here. I'll take you to court if I have to," he said, walking towards me.

"Really? Did you forget about the incident with Ryan?"

"There isn't a court in Virginia that would give you custody. You're a registered child abuser and you haven't even taken your anger management classes like the social worker ordered."

"I'll take my chances," he said.

"Go ahead. Not only will you lose…I'll make sure you never see her again. Think I'm playing? Try me!"

"You're gonna regret this, bitch, I swear you are," he taunted.

It frustrated me that he was trying to make me out to be the bad guy. If anything, I was trying to protect her from living in a home where her parents hated each other. "Look, let's do this the easy way," I told him.

"Fuck you, Zsaset," he roared, stomping from the room.

His declining demeanor warned me that I needed to leave fast. Besides, I needed to pick up my last paycheck from my job before Mrs. Bea left for the day. As I was about to leave, I noticed that Deonte had disappeared. Moments later, he re-appeared looking like a zombie. The nigga had to have been on some molly or something.

"Like I said…you can leave but Zeta is staying here with me," he said, pointing his newly purchased gun at me.

His eyes had turned blood shot red and looked to be in a satanic daze. I was scared shitless, but refused to let him know that. The realization of another man playing daddy to his daughter obviously made him snap. I swallowed hard and felt a lump forming in my throat. Quickly, I took a deep breath and got myself together. My eyes focused of the huge porcelain vase on the table that I could grab and hit his ass with when he let his guard down. One way or the other, I was leaving and taking my daughter with me.

"So, it's come to this? Really? You're going to shoot me?"

"If you try to take my daughter out of this house, I am," he shouted.

"Well, go 'head. Become a murderer. Maybe it's meant

to be."

Silence.

A complete state of eeriness filled the room.

We stood there for a few seconds staring each other down when Zeta ran over to me to show me that her dolls arm had come off. I quickly picked her up realizing my heart rate had sped up tremendously.

"I'm leaving, asshole, and I'm taking our daughter with me."

"No... you're not, Zsaset!" he yelled, as he tried to hide the gun behind his back so Zeta wouldn't see it.

"Deonte...if you try to shoot me while I have her in my arms, you might hit her. So put the gun away and just let us go before you do something you'll regret."

He put the gun away and then paced back and forth in the living room until I was ready to leave. I grabbed my purse and headed towards the door before he really lost his damn mind.

Before we left, Deonte kissed Zeta and told her he would be in Richmond to see her soon. I took one last look at the place I use to call home as I put my seat belt across my chest. The thought of leaving everyone I knew and loved saddened me. It was especially hard for me to leave Ryan and my mom. The thought of my first born not being with me really fucked with me so I made a vow to myself to at least have some fun until I had Ryan back with me and we were all a happy family, just me and my babies. So, I took a deep breath, prayed to God to give me strength, and drove off.

As I was driving out of the parking lot, I heard Deonte yelling Zeta's name and running behind my car. He had totally come unglued. When Zeta turned around and saw her dad crying and calling out to her, she started crying and kicking the back of my seat. "Daddy...I want my daddy," she yelled. She got louder and louder the further we got. Especially when she no longer saw Deonte.

I wasn't about to listen to her crying for the next hour on

the highway, so I pulled out the "Frozen" movie soundtrack I had downloaded for emergencies like this and popped into the CD player. When the music started playing, she slowly stopped sobbing. The next thing I knew she was singing her little heart as she rubbed her red swollen eyes. *Thank God for Elsa*, I thought.

• • •

When I pulled into the parking lot of the Exchange, a weird feeling that something just wasn't right came over me. Maybe it was my nerves going haywire because I was stepping outside of my comfort zone by leaving home. I shook it off, turned my car off and gathered up Zeta.

Even after stepping into the building that feeling got even more intense. I didn't want to hear anybody's mouth about my decision to quit. I'd given Mrs. Bea only a two day notice and apparently she wasn't happy about it. When Beverly, the woman behind the customer service desk, saw me she waved. Beverly was a nice woman but her hair and clothes lacked style. Her face was animated and she always had a big grin on her face like the Joker.

"Hey Zsaset. What can I do for you?" she asked.

"I'm here to get my check."

"Oh okay," she said, grabbing the big till box. She went through the envelopes but didn't see one with my name on it. "I'm gonna have to go ask Mrs. Bea where your check is because it's not in here."

"All right." Something told me bullshit was being served.

Beverly disappeared into one of the back offices and quickly returned with a grim look on her face.

"What's wrong?" I asked, placing my hands on my hips.

"Mrs. Bea would like to see you in her office."

I let out a huge sigh and then grabbed Zeta by the hand and led her into the back.

As soon as I sat down in Mrs. Bea's office I knew I was

going to have to fuck somebody up. She sat at her desk stone faced for a few seconds and then said, "Zsaset, unfortunately, I don't have a final check for you." She started fumbling around on her desk like she was looking for something. "The last couple of days that you worked your register was short. And I mean short by some large amounts."

"That's incorrect. First of all, I haven't closed in the last two weeks so whoever closed must've made a mistake."

"Well, that's possible but an anonymous person told me they overheard you telling someone that you needed extra cash."

"That's bullshit and you know it!" As I was talking, Zeta started whining which pissed me off even more. "Look, I'm not leaving here until I get my check."

"I'm not going to be able to do that because this money needs to be paid back."

I was just about to yank that bitch up when Mindy walked in smiling and talking loudly. When she saw me she stopped dead in her tracks.

"I'm sorry, I didn't know you were in with someone."

"Oh, now I see. This hoe is your anonymous source."

The two women looked at one another.

"Excuse me," Mindy said with a sneaky grin on her face.

With the quickness and without any regard I charged that bitch and rammed her into the wall. I knocked the breath out of her. Mrs. Bea's bitch ass ran out of her office to get help but it was too late. I had already commenced to beating the shit out of Mindy. In between knocking her upside the head I could hear Zeta crying, but I couldn't stop myself. It was like I was possessed. After delivering several blows to her body, I was jumped on by security. They pinned me down like they were handling a three hundred pound man. After putting plastic restraints on me they sat me down in a chair while Zeta held onto my leg crying.

"It's okay, baby. We're just playing a game," I said. "We're leaving shortly." Nothing I said comforted her. "Can you take these things off of me?" I asked one of the guards. "You're scaring my daughter."

"Zsaset, the only person scaring your daughter is you. Now, sit there and shut your trap until the MP's get here," one of the security officers stated.

The military police were a joke on our base and most of them were my old buddies from when I was in the Marines. So I was sure everything would be okay when they arrived. When the MP's showed up, all I could do was put my head down. Fuck! Recognizing one of their faces as a friend of my uncles, I knew things could get ugly. I'd promised to never embarrass him again. After all, he was a Colonel so his reputation was on the line. This time I would probably get banned from the base. I really needed to get my act together.

Before long, they'd gotten the Commanding Officer of the Exchange involved, and had of course called my uncle by phone, and one of the top Commanders on the base. They all ordered the MP to take the cuffs off of me.

Instead of being grateful for not sending my ass to jail, I blasted off, "Just give me my damn check so I can get the hell out of here."

Mrs. Bea started throwing papers everywhere in search of my paycheck. When she found it, she shoved it in my chest. I started to nuke her ass but she wasn't even worth me wasting any more time. The Commanding Officer opened the door and let me walk out. He then told the MP's everything was okay and that I was free to go. As soon as Zeta ran over to me, I picked her up and we got the hell up out of there. Although I was free to go, I realized that my uncle had pretty much written me off when I saw the look on his face when I walked out to the parking lot. He was my mom's younger brother but you would've thought he was older than her the way he tried to control her life.

"So, I guess you came to yell at me?"

"Something like that. Do you realize what an embarrassment this is for me?"

"I'm sorry, but it wasn't my fault."

"See, that's your problem. It's always someone else's fault. You never want to take responsibility for any of your destructive behavior and you're stressing your mother out. I feel sorry for that baby in your arms. It's only a matter of time before the state takes both of those kids from you."

If he wasn't my mother's brother and if I wasn't still on that damn base, I would've cussed his ass all the way out. Since I was, I got in my car and drove the fuck off.

nine...

The hour and a half trip took nearly two hours. It was my first road trip with Zeta and I had to stop several times for her to use the potty, as she liked to refer to it. I think she was still nervous from the incident at the Exchange. I'd been taking my child through too much. She deserved a little peace. I shed a little tear for Ryan at the last rest stop, when Zeta wasn't looking, and quickly put on my happy face when we got back to the car. She could sense something was up with me.

"Mommy, why are you crying," Zeta wondered.

"Zeta, don't worry about me Mommy will be okay. I just miss Ryan, that's all. He'll be with us soon."

Glancing in the rearview at my precious angel, I didn't even deserve, I could tell she was still going to worry about me and Ryan's whereabouts. I had to be extra sure to give her all my attention so she would continue to be the happy little girl she always was.

When we got to O.B's place there were several cars in the driveway. "Must be a full house," I said, turning to Zeta. She nodded her head as if she knew what I was talking about. Nervous, I walked up and rang the bell. A voice filtered from the other side of the door. "Who is it?"

"It's Zsaset," I replied.

The door swung open and I was greeted by O.B with a

big hug. "So, who do we have here?" he asked, kneeling down on one leg.

"This is my daughter, Zeta. Zeta this is mommy's friend, O.B. Can you say hello?"

"Hi," she said shyly with her fingers in her mouth.

"She's a little cutie, just like her mother," he said with a real sexy-like tone. "Nice, little curly hair."

"Thank you," she said, twirling her ponytail.

"We'll get your bags later," he told me, ushering us inside.

When I walked into the house, I found K-Dog doing what he did best, talking on the phone with his durag on. I waved to him and Quan from the living room. Zeta must have been taken back by so many men because she gripped my jacket tightly.

"It'll be okay. Mommy's here."

O.B told us to come into the kitchen to get her some juice. K-Dog walked behind us, leaving the breakfast counter where he'd been counting wads of cash.

"Hi, K-Dog."

"Hey, Zsaset," he said, as he gave me a bear hug.

"K, I told you Zsaset's gonna be stayin' with us for a while,"O.B said.

"What's a while, nigga?"

"As long as she needs, mothafucka."

"Nigga, don't get smart with me. This is my damn house. "Y'all just freeloaders," K-Dog taunted.

They all laughed and then went back to their business. O.B left out to retrieve a few bags from my car so we could prepare for bed. By the end of the night, we kicked it, watching television like we had known each other all our lives. It meant a lot to know they trusted me enough to even give me a key to the house.

The day's events had taken its toll on both Zeta and me. She was out like a light. I picked her up and we headed for bed. "You coming?" I asked, looking back at O.B

"Naw. Y'all take the bed. I'ma sleep down here."

At first I took offense then realized his reasoning. O.B felt it was best if we slept in separate bedrooms for Zeta's sake. The respect was appreciated.

I awoke the next morning only to find Zeta missing. I grabbed my robe and ran down the stairs. I walked in the kitchen and saw her sitting at the table with the guys eating breakfast. They were spoiling her rotten and she loved every minute of it. It was a relief for me to see them getting along with her. I wasn't sure how they were going to react to a baby being in the house. From the sign of things, everything was going to be all right. I guess that was because they all had small children of their own.

I cleaned the kitchen thoroughly after breakfast. It was the least I could do since they were letting me stay rent-free. I wiped the table and took Zeta upstairs to give her a bath. After settling Zeta in the tub, I turned and noticed O.B on the phone. Men could never figure out how to cover their tracks. He was whispering so low I knew he was talking to some other chick. I haven't even been here twenty-four hours and this nigga acting up, I thought. Not wanting any drama in front of Zeta, I ignored him.

I let Zeta play in the tub a while before I wrapped her in a towel and carried her in the bedroom. I couldn't believe O.B was gone. He left without saying a word. I'm gonna kill him, I thought.

I stormed down the stairs, but he was nowhere to be found. To calm my nerves, I lit a cigarette, threw on my clothes and took Zeta for a walk. I hadn't smoked in years but when I saw K-Dog's box of Newports on the table, I couldn't resist.

While we were out for our walk, I decided to try and call Ryan again. I had tried calling my mother several times but she didn't pick up. If she wasn't always in church I would've been alarmed. I left a message letting her know that I wanted to hear my sweet little man's voice and for her to call me back as soon as she got my message. I started to call my brother, but I didn't feel like hearing a damn lecture on how bad of a mother I was and how I was a big disappointment to the family…blah…blah…blah. I'm just going to enjoy the rest of my walk, I thought. I had only taken a few more steps when my phone rang. My excitement quickly turned to rage when I saw the name displayed across the screen.

"What?" I yelled.

"Let me talk to my fuckin' daughter,"

Click.

My phone immediately rang again.

"What?"

"Can I talk to my daughter?"

"Now that's more like it," I said, rolling my eyes.

I handed Zeta the phone and told her it was her daddy. Her little eyes lighting up made me feel like shit but she didn't know her daddy like I did.

I let them talk for a few minutes but I could tell from Zeta's answers that Deonte was grilling her. I grabbed the phone out of hand and told her daddy had to go.

"See, you just don't know how to act. Don't call my phone again," I said, before hanging up on him.

It was around 6:00 p.m. when O.B finally came home. He slammed the car door and ran up on the porch where I was sitting. Kneeling down, he kissed me with a nonchalant attitude.

"Why didn't you tell me you were leaving," I said still fuming.

"I told Quan to tell you," he said, pointing.

"Why didn't you tell me?"

"What difference does it make who told you?"

"That's not the point," I said, standing up.

"Look, I'm not a kid. I don't have to check in and out with you," he said. His tone and attitude totally surprised me. I wasn't ready for that. I knew this was a sure sign of trouble on the horizon.

It took me some time to calm down. His behavior totally made me rethink this whole thing. I could've stayed my ass at home if I wanted to be with someone who was going to treat me like shit. I turned to Zeta and said, "Come on baby," as I went in the house to start dinner.

Observing the sad look on my face, K-Dog asked if everything was okay. He told me that he had overheard my argument with O.B and for me not to worry about it. "He acts like that all the time. We just ignore him. For your sake, you better learn to do the same thing," he said.

By the time I finished marinating the T-bone steaks everyone was gone. *What was the point of cooking if no one was going to eat*, I thought to myself. Disappointed, I fixed Zeta and myself a plate.

We ate, cleaned up and went upstairs to get settled in for the evening. I laid her down in the spare bedroom and I went into O.B's room.

Later that night, I heard O.B creep in the room. He took his clothes off and slid in the bed. Neither one of us spoke a word. I can't believe I'm going through this shit with another man. I really should'a stayed my ass at home. That's what I get for not listening.

I turned on my side to signal that I was still awake. "What you still doin' up?" he asked.

"I couldn't sleep."

"I know somethin' that will help you sleep," he said, throwing his legs over me.

"I would prefer an apology," I said, sitting up.

"Okay, I'm sorry," he said, kissing me. "Now let me show you."

He could tell I was still upset. "Look, Boo, I'm just under a lot of stress. My wife is nagging me and these stupid ass niggas keep fuckin' up."

"What niggas?"

"I don't want to talk about that shit right now. All I want to do is make love to you," he said, leaving me naked after lifting my t-shirt over my head. O.B wasted no time handling me. He caressed my lower lips long enough to get me moist. I gazed hungrily into his eyes wanting more. He had a way of making me forget about all my worries. Before I realized, I was screaming, "Go ahead, O.B taste me, don't hold back a thing." O.B bent down and placed a wet kiss on my lips. He made his way down to my neck then my chest planting soft kisses along the way. I took my hand and clenched his rock-hard dick. I wanted to taste it in my mouth so bad but O.B pushed my hand away.

"I want it to be all about you. I want to satisfy you tonight!" he whispered in my ear.

Seconds later, he started licking and sucking both my nipples, sending sensations throughout my entire body. He then made his way down to my stomach, still kissing my body softly. Once he reached his intended target, he went in head first with his large warm tongue rotating swiftly on my clit.

"Ohhh Shittt!" I moaned, lifting my head from the pillow to witness him in action.

After only a few minutes of him pleasing me I felt myself about to cum.

"Ahhhhh, I'm about to cum!" I moaned.

"Come then baby, we got all nighttttttt!" he mumbled, palming each of my ass cheeks licking even harder.

I grabbed his head tight as my body jerked for several seconds as I experienced a huge orgasm.

O.B moaned when he felt my warm juices flowing inside his mouth.

I released my grip, collapsed, then closed my eyes thinking,

DAMN, that was the best head I've ever had. He was truly the best. He was my new addiction. However, addictions can be dangerous. I had to learn that the hard way.

ten...

The next couple of weeks with O.B were like a fairytale. It was lovemaking by morning and fancy dinners by night. We were like a little family; me, him, and Zeta. He'd even talked to Ryan over the phone a couple times.

One Saturday evening, Quan watched Zeta so we could spend some quality time together. We went for a test drive in his new Range Rover SUV then out for dinner. Halfway through our meals he got an urgent call. "I gotta take care of somethin'," he said.

"Are you gonna take me back to the house?" I asked.

"Naw, I don't have time."

This was very unusual. He never took me with him when he did business. This was one part of his life that was "off limits". Deep down, I knew what he did but I closed my eyes to it. I didn't want to believe that I could get involved with someone who sold drugs. That would absolutely break my mother's heart to know I was hanging around drug dealers. What the fuck was I thinking? I should have been spending quality time with my children, not out here in the streets. I told myself this would not last forever. I had to figure out a plan and quick.

We drove up to the Mosby Court project. "You remember this place, don't you?" he said, putting the truck in park.

"Yeah, how can I forget?"

He chuckled.

"Don't laugh, damn it. Plus, I'm feeling sick," I said, holding my stomach.

"What's wrong?"

"I think I ate something bad."

"All right, we can stop and get you somethin' after we leave."

Then I remembered I had taken a mild laxative the night before. "No, that won't be necessary."

Once we were in front of Coley's building, O.B backed the truck into a parking spot and put it in park. He reached across my leg and opened the glove compartment.

"Here, put this in your bag," he said, handing me his black Beretta.

"What do you need that for?"

"Do you see where we're at?"

I whirled around in my seat. I understood why he felt the need for protection but I just wasn't comfortable with the gun in my bag. I was so worried it would discharge prematurely and shoot me or someone else accidentally. He assured me the safety was on and I would be safe so I did what he asked. Everyone assumed because I was a marine that I was some type of gun slinger. The truth was, I only used a weapon once a year and that was for rifle qualifications. The rest of the year I sat behind a desk and handled stuff like travel and per diem. I was what you would call a paper pusher.

O.B hopped out, motioning me to follow him. I was so nervous about the people gazing at us, I walked on his heels. The group of men by the dumpster gave me the creeps. Children with snotty noses and tacky heads hung from the trees like little monkeys. The row of low brick homes reminded me of someplace out of a horror movie. It was my opinion that this place needed to be torn down immediately.

Soon, O.B led me down a short path that took us to a gray steel door. He stuck his keys in, unlocked the door, pushed it open and went in. He then quickly deactivated the alarm system. My adrenaline was pumping. Yet strangely the hint of danger turned me on.

"Wait here, I'll be back," O.B said, without even waiting for me to respond.

He disappeared into a back room. It may have been the projects on the outside, but not on the inside. A big screen television swallowed up the entire wall. Someone definitely had good taste by the looks of the fine Italian leather sofa. Moments later, a girl who was the spitting image of Chanel Iman walked out. When she saw me, she stopped dead in her tracks.

"Who the hell are you?" she asked.

I didn't immediately answer so she said, "Excuse me...why are you in my house?"

"Oh, I'm Zsaset. I'm here with O.B"

"Oh so you're, Zsaset. I was beginning to think you were ugly or somethin'," she said with a smirk.

Of course I wasn't amused so I just inhaled and exhaled deeply to let her know she was getting on my damn nerves.

"I'm Lina, Coley's girlfriend. Anyway. So you're supposed to be O.B's girl, huh?" she said, taking a seat in the chair across from where I stood.

"Not supposed to be...I am his girl." Of course I rolled my eyes to let her know I didn't give a fuck how she felt about me.

She gave me a yeah right look then said, "Ummm, hmmn, if you say so."

Just as I was about to ask her what she meant, O.B emerged from the back room with a scruffy short guy.

"Zsaset, this is Coley."

"Coley, this is my shorty, Zsaset."

After we exchanged greetings, O.B pulled me down a narrow hallway into a small bedroom. I couldn't believe my eyes. Cash was stacked neatly and high, like money in a bank vault. The moment my eyes saw the two money machines, I knew O.B wasn't just small time.

"Where did all this money come from?" I asked.

"You know exactly where it came from."

I tried to act like I didn't know what he was talking about. But it was evident he was on to me.

"So, I guess I was right about you."

"I guess you were," he said.

"I know you probably don't approve of my methods, but I have a kid to feed. I gotta do what I gotta do."

"I understand what you're saying, but why don't you just get a job?"

He laughed, "Who's gonna give me a job with my rap sheet."

"Driving without a license is not that serious," I said, referring to the reason he told me he spent a little time in jail.

"Either you are really naive or you're a good faker. You know that? Driving without a license is the least of my crimes. But we won't get into that."

What the hell did he mean by that? Right at that moment, I knew my fairytale was coming to an end.

"Look, I just wanted to come clean. I'm tired of trying to hide this shit from you. I'm tired of getting into fights because I can't tell you where I'm going in the middle of the night. It was really starting to get to me, Boo."

After listening to him, I kissed his lips and promised to love him no matter what. I wanted to continue our conversation but I was starting to get a case of the bubble guts again.

"Oh God," I said, squeezing my butt cheeks together. "I need to use the bathroom."

O.B started laughing. "The bathroom is straight across the hall."

"This shit ain't funny!" I yelled, running to the bathroom.

I could hear him still laughing as I struggled to get my jeans down and put toilet tissue all over the seat of the toilet. No offense but I didn't know these people; especially that trick, Lina.

It felt so good to relieve myself. By the time I was done,

I found myself wiping my ass way too many times, but was halted by the sound of men shouting for everyone to get on the floor. I thought maybe it was the police at first, but when I heard the way they were speaking, I knew O.B and his friends were being robbed.

My heart raced and I couldn't think straight. I wasn't sure if they knew I was there, so I knew not to flush the toilet. I could tell there were at least two of them by the different tones in their voices. As I stood by the door, I heard one of them asking if anyone else was in the house. O.B quickly answered, "No."

There was so much commotion going on I wasn't sure what I should do until I heard O.B say, "Everything's cool. Just don't move."

I thought maybe he was talking to Lina but she wasn't screaming or upset. He's talking to me, I thought.

I softly stepped into the bathtub and pulled the shower curtain back just in case they came in the bathroom. Right then and there, I started praying to God. When I sat my purse down, it was slightly open enough for me to see that I had O.B's gun. I pulled it out and took it off safety as my hands trembled. Since I couldn't hold a steady hand, I had to hold it with both hands.

My heart raced faster when I heard one of the gunmen ordering Coley to put the money in bags and the other gunman ordering O.B and Lina to get on their knees. When Coley wouldn't comply, a struggle began.

I heard a gun go off.

Sweat poured from my head as I listened intently.

"Yo son, just keep cool," O.B said trying to take control of the situation.

I slowly pulled the bathroom door inward just enough to peek outside. When I saw Coley lying on the floor bleeding and a gun at my man's head that's when I sprang into action. I couldn't let O.B die because I was too afraid to use the gun. My balls grew. I swung the door open and starting spraying bullets like I was Keisha from New Jack City. I was so nervous I was hitting the ceiling, the walls and the furniture. I got one of the gunmen in the head, the other gunmen in the chest even though I wasn't even aiming in those spots.

"Zsaset...Zsaset, stop shooting!" O.B yelled, with one hand in the air and the other one covering his head.

I immediately dropped the gun and held my face when I saw the lifeless bodies lying on the floor. O.B ran over and asked me if I was okay while Lina ran to Coley's aid. Miraculously, he was only shot in the arm.

O.B hadn't stopped pacing since he got up. He knew it was only a matter of time before the police got there so he started throwing the money and money machines into bags.

"Zsaset, help me," he yelled, jerking me out of my trance.

He handed me two of the bags while Coley instructed Lina what to do.

"Son, you gonna be all right?" O.B asked Coley with the straps of two bags hefted onto his shoulder

"Yeah, y'all just get the fuck outta here. I'll take care of everythin'."

At a fast pace, O.B and I walked down the sidewalk and loaded the bags into the Range Rover while cautiously looking around for signs of the cops. It was so dark I couldn't even see if anyone was watching us.

As I jumped into the passenger seat, I could hear sirens blaring. O.B got into the truck, and started the engine. As he pulled out, the Rover lunged backward. He didn't slow down until we reached the end of the block where police cars were approaching. After they passed us his foot slammed back onto the accelerator and we headed away from the scene of the crime. Once we were close to home and there were no signs of the police, I laid my head against the head rest and let out a heavy sign. The image of the two dead men on the floor was etched into my brain. *What the hell have I got myself into*, I thought. I was sure I was going to jail for the rest of my life. O.B on the other hand was cool as a cucumber. I guess he had more faith in

Coley and Lina than I did.

When we walked through the door, K-Dog and Quan were sitting on the couch watching television and Zeta was in the bed sleep. There was a six pack of beer and a pizza box sitting on the coffee table. O.B fell back in the chair.

"What the hell is wrong with you?" Quan asked.

"Man, y'all ain't gonna believe what just happened."

While he told them our deadly ordeal, I went upstairs and sprawled across the bed. I felt really bad about having to kill those guys. I also felt a little guilty that I cared more about what this meant for my life. My actions not only affected me, they affected my friends and family. Damn, how old were they? What if they were kids? I would never take another person's life but like I always say, "If it comes down to me or them. I'm not going down without a fight." I tried to wrap my brain around what I had done. What if Coley and Lina broke down and snitched on me? I wondered how long it would be before the cops got there to arrest me for murder. Who would take care of Zeta? I just couldn't believe this shit was happening. I needed to confide in someone so I picked up the phone to call my girl, Brina. She was the only one I could trust.

Danette Majette

eleven...

Days after the shooting, the news coverage in Richmond had died down because there were bigger and better stories going on. Coley had somehow gotten the police to believe there were three robbers originally, and one turned on the other two robbers; killing them both and shooting Coley. I had to give it them they were good at getting out of sticky situations.

My guilt had started to subside once I got it through my head that I saved us all from being killed. O.B kept giving me different scenarios of how things could've turned out if I hadn't been in that bathroom. He and Coley seemed to think I was a hero, nothing had been spoken about what Lina thought.

Feeling like a hero wasn't a bad thing, but I wasn't however feeling good about O.B and I. Our relationship was slowly deteriorating. It all started with late night calls that had O.B running in and out of the house. Some days I didn't see him at all. Talking about it always led to big blowouts. I wasn't about to go through the same bullshit I went through with Deonte always arguing, so I let O.B do his thang. If he didn't care about spending time with me, the goal was for me to wean myself off of him.

To keep myself from getting lonely and bored, I spent my time spending his cash. Brina and Sheba said I had nothing to trip about, but to me, happiness reigned over money. I also used his money to redecorate their four bedroom townhouse. It went from a boring, bachelor-looking pad to a gorgeous place fitting the life styles of the rich and famous. I had to admit, I had skills when it came to decorating and probably should have become an interior designer. O.B was very impressed.

Summer time was here and it brought out the best in me. My spirits were high. I'd just finished talking to my mom about bringing Ryan up to see me the following weekend. She agreed which had me on cloud nine. Damn, I missed my lil man. Being without him left a void in my heart.

I slid on a pair of booty shorts and started cleaning up the room I shared with O.B I hooked up my iPhone speaker and sang along to "Flawless" by Beyoncé as I cleaned. Every few minutes I would go check on my baby girl, Zeta in the next room as she played with the huge doll house K-Dog bought her. She loved that thing and would play quietly by herself for hours.

I was folding up the last of the laundry when I heard O.B, K-Dog and Quan talking loud downstairs as they entered the apartment. Seconds later the lyrics by the rapper Drake, "*Started from the bottom now we here!*" blasted from the Bose sound system downstairs, drowning out my music. I put up the rest of the clothes and told Zeta I would be right back and headed downstairs. O.B had promised we would spend some time together, and to me, today seemed like the perfect day. Once I reached downstairs, I stood in the doorway of the kitchen, unnoticed, watching them put large amounts of cash into several money counting machines on the kitchen table.

"O.B, can I speak to you for a second?" I yelled, over the loud music.

O.B got up and walked towards me trying to block my view of what they were doing.

But it was too late. I'd already witnessed K-Dog put a stack of the money in a bag.

"I'm gonna go take care of that thang, be right back," he informed O.B

O.B nodded his head.

Needing a break, Quan pushed the rest of the money to the side of the table and covered it and the machines with a sheet before heading outside to smoke a cigarette.

Once the house was clear, O.B looked in my direction.

"What up, Zsa?" he asked, irritated.

"Can we please spend some time together today, you know, go someplace, see a movie?"

"I can't today. I got business to handle but tomorrow we'll do whatever you like."

I was pissed that he was blowing me off again. I also knew that his promise for spending time the next day was probably a lie, too. He walked into the kitchen and reached under the sheet and grabbed some money and handed it to me.

"Here, you and Zeta go enjoy yourself today."

I grabbed the money and smiled. It was roughly three grand. Cash always seemed to make things better; even if it was only temporary. O.B grabbed me tight and pulled me close, looking deep into my eyes.

"You are so sexy and classy. You know you my baby, right?"

I smiled. Something about him made me weak. We held each other tightly while passionately kissing for at least two minutes straight. The feeling was so intense I wanted to pull his jeans down and jump on his dick.

Minutes later, we were interrupted by Quan.

"Yo man, I just saw Yaya pulling into the parking lot!"

O.B pushed me away as if he didn't even know me. His demeanor quickly changed.

"What the fuck she doin' here? Go stall her!"

Quan took off outside and O.B ran in the kitchen. It was weird seeing him so disheveled. He was always the calm, level-headed one when it came to handling problems. I watched as he took the money machines off the table shoving them under the cabinet, slamming doors in the process. He scooped all the money into the sheet, tossed it across his back and ran upstairs at top speed.

"Zsa, come help me move your shit!"

I stood puzzled for a second wondering what was going

on and who the hell was Yaya.

Once I got in the bedroom, I saw O.B taking my things out of his room into the spare bedroom.

"What's going on? Why you moving my stuff?"

"My wife is here. So please act like you K-Dog's girl. I don't need no problems from her right now. Help me get the rest of your stuff outta my room now, Zsa!" he yelled.

I didn't like it, but I helped move the rest of my things, upset and confused. When we finished, O.B left me and went back downstairs. I was in my feelings and started to just stay in the spare bedroom to avoid the whole scene, but curiosity got the best of me. I grabbed Zeta and decided to play along. We both headed down to check out O.B's wife.

When I reached the living room, K-Dog was back and all three friends sat on the couch discussing and preparing like something bad was about to happen. Suddenly, there was a knock at the door. I put Zeta down on the chair and proceeded to answer it until I was stopped by O.B

"Zsa, wait listen, I already explained that my wife has a lot on me, and I can't afford to end things with her right now. So, please go along with the plan for me!" he whispered.

The knocking at the door got louder.

"Whatever, O.B!" I said, sitting down next to K-Dog.

"Open this muthufuckin' door," the irate voice sounded.

"Quan, go answer the door. Here comes the bullshit!" O.B said, taking a deep breath.

When Quan opened the door, I was absolutely caught off guard with what I saw step inside. *This can't be his wife,* I thought to myself. This hood rat had blue and black braids in her hair, a small blue tee shirt, a pair of colorful leggings and some timberland boots. For a second, I thought it was Shanaynay from the Martin show. She looked around the room before speaking. I could tell by her facial expression she was impressed by my upgrades to the place. Still, she had a Lisa Bonet face and Kim-K stature. I could see how he fell for her.

"What up, hubby?" she said, placing her hand on her hip.

88

"What you doing here, Yaya?" he asked.

She ignored him and spoke to K-Dog and Quan.

They spoke back to her acting like they were watching TV.

"Oh yeah, Quan, don't think I didn't see your punk ass run in the house to tell O.B I was outside, you little Chinese looking fucker!"

"Whatever Yaya, you just got here and already trippin'!" Quan snapped back, as he got up to leave. K-Dog decided to leave, too. They both went to take care of business so they wouldn't have to deal with her. I picked up Zeta and was just about to go up to K-Dogs' room to make myself scarce when O.B's wife stopped me.

"And who might you be?" she asked me with attitude.

"I'm Zsa!" I replied.

"Oh so this is Zsa? Umm hum," she said, walking around me like I was a piece of meat. "Nothing like the description you gave me of her O.B. She is cute. And what lie did you tell me again? She fuck with K-Dog or is she one of your workers? I can't remember."

"We already discussed this like 50 times, Yaya, so chill," O.B told her.

"I'm no worker!" I blurted out.

She smirked, flashing her large wedding ring in my face.

"Well, let me introduce myself. I'm Yashika, O.B's wife, the mother of his son and the head bitch in charge!"

Blow it out your ass cause ain't nobody trying to hear that bullshit, I thought as I walked away from her, headed up to K-Dogs room.

By the time we made it upstairs, fire damn near exploded from my nose. I hated her and I hated O.B for putting me through that. It didn't take long for K-Dog's sensitive side to kick in. He said all the right things to ease my pain as we both heard O.B and Yaya come upstairs and settle in for the night. I was lying at one end of the bed and K-Dog was lying at the other end while we talked for hours. It was so creepy, yet comforting, being in bed with O.B's friend even if it was for show.

I tossed and turned for an hour, trying to drown out the sound of O.B and his ghetto fabulous wife having sex in the next room. He claimed he didn't want to be with her but it sounded like he was sure fucking her extra good.

"Yessss, yesss, give it to me daddy... this my dick!" he yelled as loud as she could. "Deeper baby, deeeeeppper... Damn....That's what I'm talkin' bout. You givin' Yaya all this dick," she bragged.

His wife was yelling and moaning like it was the best dick in the world. I had to admit, he could put it down in the bed, but she was real extra with the shit. Probably doing it on purpose to piss me off and it was working. I put the pillow over my head to drown out Yaya yelling, O.B's grunts and the pounding against the wall. It was as if I could feel each hump he was giving her. It was driving me crazy. My pussy got wet thinking about the way he looked into my eyes, and grabbed my hair before he dug deep inside me. Now he was   giving dick to that ratchet bitch!

I didn't like being disrespected, and it was taking everything in me not to go in there and beat that bitch down and claim my man. But instead I kissed Zeta on the forehead as she slept and left the spare bedroom and went downstairs.

Once downstairs, I turned on the TV and watched an old episode of Scandal. About an hour later, I dozed off until I felt O.B tapping me. He had come downstairs to get a drink of water.

"Zsa, baby, are you ok?" he whispered.

I looked at him standing over me in a pair of basketball shorts with sweat decorated on his bare chest. Instantly, I rolled my eyes. Hurt filled me.

"What you think, O.B? I just listened to you fuck your wife!"

"Just bear with me. She'll be gone tomorrow, and I promise I will make it up to you!"

A tear rolled down my cheek and I quickly wiped it

away. I didn't want him to see me cry.

"You think it's just that easy, huh?" I huffed.

"I told you, I don't have a choice. She used to work for me and knows everything about my operation and has threatened to go to the Feds if I divorce her. This shit ain't no joke!"

I could see the hurt in O.B's eyes. But I still couldn't help the way I felt. This shit was straight Jerry Springer and I wasn't feeling it at all. O.B looked over his shoulder and quickly moved away from me when he heard Yaya coming down the stairs wearing a black bathrobe.

"Well...well...well, what do we have here? You down here talkin' to the help? Y'all wouldn't happen to be dis-cussing these pink thongs I found in your bed, would you?" she asked, holding them up in the air.

O.B didn't respond so she directed her attention to me.

"Are you fuckin' my husband #9?"

I glanced at O.B thinking, no this bitch didn't just hit me with a line from Tyler Perry's *The Have and Have Not's*. I stood up and walked towards her. I was sick of her ass.

"Let me tell you something...," I blurted out.

O.B saw the rage in my eyes and put up the praying position with his hands behind her back. I took a deep breath and decided not to tell Yaya the truth even though I felt she already knew.

"Listen Yaya, I don't know what you're talking about, but I'm sick of your ass. I don't want your husband so stay the fuck away from me."

K-Dog was listening at the top of the stairs and decided to help me out.

"Come to bed, Zsaset!" he yelled down the steps.

Hearing him call me to bed threw me off for a moment. It sounded sweet on my ears. I needed to play it off, and wanted to stick it to O.B so I yelled, "I'm coming, baby!"

O.B snarled as I walked away.

As soon as I entered K-Dog's room, I collapsed on the bed beside him. When K-Dog saw the tears building up in my eyes, he reached over and hugged me.

"Come on, baby girl. Don't cry, you know how this game goes."

I snuggled in his arms and fought back the tears.

A few minutes later, I heard Yaya and O.B arguing as they were approaching the top of the stairs. Yaya was de-mending that he put me out the house.

"I'm serious, nigga! Go in there right now and put her out! Her and her nappy head daughter!"

"I'm not doing that, Ya! I told you, she's K-Dog's girl." I heard him say submissively.

I snuggled up closer into K-Dog's arms in bed on purpose when I heard them coming since our door was wide open. I looked up as they passed K-Dog's doorway.

I could tell O.B didn't like what he saw. Jealously showed all over his face.

Yaya however, had a large wicked grin on her face. I looked at her thinking; we'll see who has the last laugh, bitch!

# twelve...

The next morning, I got up early and started breakfast. Reaching into the refrigerator, I slid Yaya's sixteen ounce bottle of Coca Cola to the side that she had been using to mix her liquor. I got what I needed out and closed the door. With my hand still on the handle, I opened it back up.

A light bulb lit up in my head. I ran up to the bathroom and grabbed my Miralax, quickly returning to the kitchen. I took the bottle of Coke, opened it and poured some of the Miralax inside. Thinking of them having sex made me mad so I emptied the bottle into the soda with a big smirk on my face. As I was tightening the bottles I could hear footsteps coming down the stairs. I put the Coke back in the fridge but I couldn't find a hiding spot for the Miralax so I hid it in the trash.

"Mommy, I'm hungry," Zeta said, rubbing her eyes.

"Well, good because mommy made you chocolate chip pancakes."

"Yaay!" She said, perking up immediately.

I made us a plate and sat down to eat. Minutes later, Yaya walked into the kitchen beaming like she was on her honeymoon.

"Good morning! What's your name again?" she said with a sneer.

"Zsaset," I said, returning the sneer.

She opened the refrigerator and grabbed her soda. Chugging it all up, she threw the bottle away and returned upstairs to get dressed. *Oh shit, I didn't know she was to drink the whole thing*, I thought.

Not even an hour later, I heard a loud thump as I was trying to organize my clothing that O.B had thrown all over the place. It was Yaya literally falling into the bathroom, trying to get to the toilet. I grabbed a pillow and smothered my face into it.

"What you laughin' at?" K-Dog asked, peeking from his bathroom. I kept laughing as the sounds of moans and groans came from the guest bathroom. I motioned for him to come here. K-Dog walked over to the door. When he heard Yaya screaming for dear life, he fell on the floor in laughter.

"What did you do?' he whispered.

I leaned over and whispered back what I did. He started laughing even harder then. His eyes were tearing up by now because he couldn't stand her evil ass either. We both fell into each other's arms hysterically laughing. Our eyes met and for a moment I felt so connected to him I almost felt myself wanting to kiss him.

I jumped back, realizing that we could never cross that line.

Hours later, K-Dog and I were sitting on the couch watching Best Man Holiday movie when the scene of them finding out Mia had cancer was on. We both were so emotionally drawn into the movie we hadn't even noticed the hateful glares we were getting from O.B and Yaya. I took my head and laid it on K-Dog's chest and for a second it felt like our hearts were beating as one.

K-Dog was the kind of man I should've been with. He was the exact opposite of O.B Even though I didn't owe O.B anything, I would never mess with his boy like that. I especially wouldn't want to do anything to hurt my girl Brina. She and K-Dog had been messing around with each other off and on for years. For some reason, they could never make it work because of the distance between them with K-Dog being in Richmond and Brina being in Norfolk. Brina was also not his type.

O.B was on Yaya's heels trying to get the bitch out of there, but she kept bending over because she was still having pains in her stomach.

"Are you gonna be able to drive?" O.B asked like a whimp as he sat her bag down.

"Yeah. I got it. I'm a soldier. Soldiers handle things," she stated, giving me a side-eye.

Once she got herself together, O.B opened the door and they walked out to the car. As soon as the door closed behind him, K-Dog and I fell out laughing.

"I told that bitch I was going to get the last laugh," I said, barely able to talk.

When O.B walked back in he was furious.

"What did you do? Cause I know you did something."

I looked at K-Dog. "What you lookin' at him for? I'm talkin' to you."

With an offended look on my face I answered, "I have no idea what you're talking about."

"Yes, you do. I know you did something to my wife. That's fucked up."

I jumped to my feet. "You wanna talk fucked up. You pawning me off on your friend, throwing my clothes into another room, letting your wife talk to me like I was some whore on the streets, and fucking her in the next room knowing I would be able to hear you. That's fucked up."

"Yo, you knew what it was when we first got together. So stop playin' the victim. As a matter of fact, I'm done with your spoiled ass, man. I ain't got time for this bullshit."

"Really? You're done with me? I've been done with your ass!"

Tired of talking, I ran up the stairs yelling, "I'll be out of your house tomorrow."

"You do that, bitch!"

Gathering my belongings, I cried for being so stupid. Uprooting myself and my child must've ranked in the top five dumbest things I'd ever done. With tears still streaming, I stuffed my last pair of jeans in the bag with nowhere to go. The next few hours passed by quickly. I sat on the edge of the bed wondering how and why I fell so hard for O.B.

I think I was attracted to his bad boy image. Perhaps he brought some excitement to my life. Especially since my life before him had been so boring. One thing was for sure. Men are like jeans. Some of them fit well and some don't. Exhausted from trying to figure out what went wrong, I crawled in the bed with my baby and cried myself to sleep.

Zeta woke me up the next morning with tons of tiny, wet kisses. It was just what I needed. She dragged me downstairs for breakfast. As soon as my foot hit the first step I heard O.B snapping at K-Dog and Quan like a madman. He gave me a look that almost made my heart stop when I sat at the table. That nigga had kill in his eyes. I didn't understand it.

"What the fuck you looking at?" he asked.

I looked behind me to see if there was someone else there, but there wasn't.

"Are you talking to me?" I asked, feeling like I wanted to fight.

"Who do you think I'm talking to?"

K-Dog warned me about his attitude but I wasn't prepared for this. "Wait a minute, why do you have an attitude with me?"

"You know why?" he said, then walked out the door.

I stood motionless a few seconds before I sat back down. I tried to block the whole ugly scene out of my head, but it was useless. It replayed in my head like a scratched CD.

K-Dog sat down to comfort me. He tried telling me corny jokes but it didn't work. My emotions got the best of me. Before I knew it, I was balling.

"It's gonna be all right, ZsaZsa."

"What did you call me?"

"Zsa Zsa. That's my new name for you. Zsa Zsa Gabor

was a bad bitch. She would never let a man get to her. So, Zsa Zsa, get yourself together, and go put on your clothes. We're going to the mall."

That's why I loved K-Dog. Within minutes, my crying turned into laughter. K-Dog always had the gentle kind of humor that took away my pain.

After he saw that I was feeling better, he ran upstairs to change. Moments later, I ran up behind him.

At the top of the stairs, I observed K-Dog consulting with Zeta about what she should wear. He had a great rapport with her. I think it was because he acted like a kid himself. Not in a negative way, in a free spirited way. He was always the life of the party and he never let anything get him down. I admired him for that.

When we got to the mall, K-Dog bought Zeta something from every children's store there. Then it was my turn. We headed to Lady Foot Locker.

"Yeah, I'll take this in an eight," I told the sales clerk, pointing to the pair of construction Timberlands displayed on the wall.

"What about Zeta?" K-Dog asked.

"What about her? Don't you think she's has enough stuff?" "Well, that's where you're wrong young lady. She needs to have these and these and these."

"What?" I said.

I could tell by the way the clerk sprinted to the stockroom that she was elated. She had a sale for six pairs of shoes and she didn't even have to break a sweat.

As she rung up our purchase, I saw an accepting applications sign on the counter. Great. I can get a job here. I waited for the clerk to complete our transaction before I inquired about the positions they had open.

"We have a full-time position open. Are you interested?" "Yes," I replied.

"Okay, all you have to do is go online and enter this store number. If you want, I'll put in a good word for you."

"You'll do that for me?"

"After the sale you just gave me, you better believe it." She gave me a business card with the stores information on it and then handed me our bags. "Thank you," she said.

"No, thank you."

I pulled out my Samsung Galaxy and began filling out the application as we sat down in the food court to eat. "Zsaset, why you trying to get a job?" K-Dog asked.

I explained to him that I needed to move out because my relationship with O.B was over and I needed to get my own place.

"You know you can stay with us, right."

"Do you really think O.B would let me stay in his house?"

"If it was his house ...probably not. But since the house in question is mine, I really don't think he has any say-so about the matter."

"What," I said confused. "You mean to tell me that's your house."

"Every nook and cranny. I own it."

I felt relieved.

"Don't you remember what I said to him when you first moved in? I wasn't playing. That is my house and they are free-loaders."

I had forgotten all about that. K-Dog offered Zeta and me to stay. My prayers were answered. The power O.B had over me was gone.

"K-Dog, I don't know why you are so nice to me and Zeta but I want you to know that I really do appreciate it. If there's anything you need ..."

K-Dog cut me off. "Zsaset, it ain't no thing. I ain't helpin' you out so you can do somethin' for me. Let's just say you remind me of someone that was special to me, that I lost."

"Would I be prying to ask who?" K-Dog was quiet for a minute and he swallowed hard. He started to speak a couple of times and stopped.

Finally he said, "My sister...she was killed a couple of years ago by some niggas that were looking for me."

"I'm sorry, K-Dog." He shook his head.

I tried to lighten the mood a little. "K, I'll be your sister if you'll be my brother. My real brother is a stuffed shirt, know-it-all, so I would prefer you over him any day."

K-Dog smiled and extended his hand. "Deal, sis." We shook on it.

I examined the application one last time before I submitted it.

"I'm gonna go let her know I did the application already," I said.

K-Dog sat outside the store with Zeta just in case they wanted to interview me on the spot.

"If they need help that bad they might hire you today," he said.

He was right. The manager, Larry interviewed me as soon as I went back in. He asked me a few questions like did I have any experience in sales and what hours I was available to work. He then offered me the position. Of course, I graciously accepted.

I switched from the back and gave the clerk a wink. I figured it was because of her I got the job. I ran over to K-Dog and told him the great news.

"They even want me to start tomorrow," I added. Then it hit me that I didn't have a babysitter. "K-Dog, do you know anyone who baby-sits in the neighborhood?"

"Yeah, the lady next door but she won't be back until tomorrow."

"Oh God." Now what am I going to do?

"Don't worry. I'll watch Zeta for you." Grateful, I gave him a big hug and kiss. "Don't worry about it," he said.

Things were starting to look up for me. However, I had a feeling danger was looming around the corner.

 thirteen...

We walked through the door and threw our bags on the couch. O.B walked out of the kitchen and got in my face. "What the hell you still doin' here?" he barked.

In my mind I had jumped on his ass and beat the shit out of him. This dude was something else. He just had no idea who he was messing with. I was not about to let him spoil my day so I just laughed at him.

"I'll let K-Dog tell you why," I sneered, as I ran up the stairs.

I was unpacking my last box when I heard O.B ranting and raving. Curious, I went to see what was going on. I was on the last step when I heard K-Dog telling O.B the good news. It was good news for me anyway.

"Look man, just because you have a problem with her doesn't mean I do. I'm not about to put her and her baby out in the streets, so get over it," K-Dog said. "She staying until she gets her own place."

"This is some bullshit, man!" O.B screamed. "You know there is no way in hell we can stay in the same house."

"Come on, man. Yes, you can. We'll be one big happy family," K-dog said with laughter.

O.B was so vexed he started lashing out at me the moment my foot hit the last step.

"You think you slick usin' your baby so you can stay

here," he said.

"I didn't have to use my baby. K-Dog cares about me and Zeta," I countered.

"Well guess what? I'll let you in on somethin'. I don't care.
I never did."

His words shot through me like a bullet. Not only did he accuse me of using my child to get what I wanted, he had the nerve to say he didn't care about us when he was the one who told me to move to Richmond in the first place. Before I knew it, I clawed him like a wild cat. He staggered back into the wall and immediately clutched his face. The anger in his eyes was a sure sign that I was in trouble. As I took off to run, he slapped me across my face sending me tumbling towards the couch. Then he grabbed me by the arms and shook me so hard that spit flew out of my mouth. "What the ...!" I screamed. Out the corner of my eye, I saw K-Dog standing behind O.B pulling him off of me.

"Mannnnnn, come on," K-Dog told him, "You know we don't hit women."

"Fuck her!" he retorted.

This nigga sunk to an all-time low by hitting me. Granted, I did scratch him. But for him to' hit me just showed me what kind of man he really was.

"Yo son, that was uncalled for," K-Dog said, pushing him into the kitchen.

"Fuck that bitch. I should kill her ass for scratchin' my face," O.B yelled.

"Go ahead, mothafucka. Do it," I challenged.

"Fuck you," he yelled again.

"Fuck me? You wish! That shit will never happen again! And your sex was never really good. I was faking, nigga!"

I couldn't crush his heart with words so I went for the next best thing, his ego. He lunged at me again but K-Dog stopped him just in time. I was so mad, I forgot all about my child so I ran upstairs to check on her. She was on the bed with

her face buried in a pillow screaming and crying. I tried to calm
her down. I rubbed her back and told her that everything was
going to be all right. At that very moment she asked me to call
her father.

A few minutes later, K-Dog came in the room.

"Y'all all right?" he asked, sitting on the edge of the bed.

"Yeah, but I have to move out. I promised myself that I
would never let another man hit me."

"Understood, but don't let O.B run you out of here. Trust
me, he'll never put his hands on you again. All you have to do is
stay out of his way. Then again, there are a few other issues you
need to dodge at the moment."

K-Dog's demeanor changed. I could tell something serious was bothering him. "What? Tell me?"

"I got a call just before you came downstairs. Word on
the street is that some detectives are looking for you about those
dudes you smoked."

I froze. It was almost as if every other word K-Dog
spoke sounded muffled and foreign. I sat in a daze for seconds
before snapping out of it. "I'm going to jail?" I asked nervously.

"Hell nah! For some reason, one of the detectives didn't
believe Coley's story so they been conducting a thorough investigation. Lina broke under pressure and said there was a girl
that came by that day. She didn't give them your real name
though."

Hives welled up on my skin. I knew Lina didn't like me
and had no reason to save my ass.

"So, how do you know it's me they're looking for?"

"They walking 'round Mosby Court with a sketch of
you. They confiscated the cameras and although your face was
blurry, they were able to compile a sketch. Come on, Zsa. It's
been all over the news and you know how this *First 48* shit
works. Folks say it looks sorta like you, so somebody snitch-
ing."

I trembled as if I'd already been convicted.

"Nobody knows it's you Zsaset, and O.B got rid of the

gun, so you're good. Nobody even knows you around there. Niggas will say anything if they think a cash reward coming their way," K-Dog stated with confidence.

My head began to throb. Thoughts of being handcuffed in front of Zeta filled my mind. I was so pissed at O.B getting me into this trouble but I only had myself to blame. I should've listened to my mother and Brina and stayed my monkey ass at home. Why did I think being in the middle of a drug transaction was okay?

I sat with my face in my hands for almost an hour, trying to compose my thoughts. Not only did O.B break up with me, tried to throw me and my daughter out on the streets, but now the police were looking for me because of him. If it wasn't for me, his ass would probably be dead right now. I risked my life and my freedom for the bitch ass nigga, and now I might be going to jail?

For the second night in a row, I cried myself to sleep.

● ● ●

Wanting to make a good impression, I arrived fifteen minutes early to work the next day. I walked in and was greeted by the clerk from the day before.

"Hi, so are you excited about your first day?" she said.

"Yeah, but I'm a little nervous."

"There's nothing to be nervous about, you'll be all right. By the way, my name is Vicki," she said, extending her hand.

"My name is Zsaset."

"I know. Larry told me."

She helped me fill out my paperwork then told me about the company's policies. We talked before the store opened and she gave me the low down on all the employees. I got a crash course on how to work the hustlers that came in and what to do if I had any problems with the girls from the projects. What Vicki didn't know was that I could school her on both topics because I was already a pro.

The first two hours, I trained with Vicki I watched how she handled the customers. She had skills. She could sell a bald-headed woman barrettes. I was amazed at how she convinced customers to buy shit they didn't even need. That pumped me up to want to jump right into the game.

I noticed Larry watching closely as I helped a customer with some shoes. After the young lady with red hair and a pink Nike sweat-suit left, Larry came over to me smiling.

"Good job, Zsaset. I like the fact that you suggested socks with the lady's shoes. If you like, you can go to lunch."

I couldn't wait to sit down so I made the short trip around the corner to the food court. After ordering my food, I noticed two guys fighting in the back of the food court near the restrooms. *Are you fuckin' kidding me? I don't have time for this bullshit*, I thought to myself. I was hungry and I didn't want anything getting in the way of me eating. All of a sudden, I saw one guy pull out a gun and start firing while running backwards. The other guy started firing back. They both fired several shots at one another in the crowded food court as hundreds of pan-icked shoppers sprinted for the exits. All of a sudden a herd of people ran toward me screaming, running and freaking out. Two people were even trampled on. Of course, I never panicked or moved. I knew what I was getting into before I took the job.

The mall, which was popular with teenagers, was soon evacuated. Unbelievable, I said to myself as I made my way to safety. Seconds later, Vicki and Larry joined me in the parking lot as we waited for word to return back to work. Police and paramedics were on the scene quickly. Swarms of people watched as an injured man with visible bullet wounds was wheeled out on a stretcher.

"Hey did you see the guys that were shooting?" Vicki asked.

"Yes, but I was too busy trying to get the hell out of there to get a really good description."

"Well, don't even tell the police that. You don't want people to think you're a snitch."

If this bitch tell me one more thing about what to do and not to do in Richmond I was going to take her damn head off. I had only been in Richmond for a short amount of time and I was already getting tired of it. After about two hours we were allowed to go back inside. We just weren't allowed to go through the food court doors or near the area of the shootings. That was the first time I had actually seen a shootout. Little did I know I would see more and even be involved in one myself.

● ● ●

Anxious to find a permanent babysitter, I walked next door once I got off that evening to see if our neighbor was back from her trip. The door opened, and a large-framed, white woman greeted me. Her beautiful smile overpowered her weight.

"Hello, I'm Zsaset," I said, extending my hand.

"Oh, are you Zeta's mom?"

"Yes, I am." She welcomed me in and I took a seat on the fluffy couch. Her house was beautifully decorated in a shabby chic decor.

"So, what can I do for you?" she asked.

"I was wondering if you could baby-sit my daughter while I work?"

"Sure, I would love to. Your daughter is such a sweetheart." "Thank you. You've met her already?"

"She was out on your patio earlier watching my kids play in the pool. I asked if she wanted to join them and she said, 'Yes,' but the gentleman watching her said she should wait until you got home."

I was a little relieved to hear her say that. Zeta was shy. I tried several times to get her to go out and play with some of the other kids but she wouldn't.

"I know its short notice, but can you start tomorrow?"

"No problem," she said.

It was settled. I finally had a full-time babysitter.

I walked to the house, stuck my key in the door and turned the knob. Hearing Zeta screaming, "Mommy, Mommy you're home," made me forget how badly my feet hurt.

"Were you a good girl today?"

She nodded her head yes and then gave me a big hug and kiss.

"I don't know why mommy even asked you that. You're always a good girl," I said, as I took my shoes off.

The smell of fried chicken lured me into the kitchen.

"I hope you're hungry because I'm cooking up a storm," K-Dog said.

He wasn't lying either. He was cooking a Sunday dinner on a Tuesday.

"So, how was your first day?"

"It was cool until some fools started shooting in the food court."

"Yo' these country ass Richmond niggas be wildin' out."

"Yeah, I thought I left that hood shit in Norfolk. But other than that...work was good. I guarantee you in a couple of weeks I'll be running the joint," I said with confidence.

"I know you will."

"No more talk about that shit in Mosby, right?" My heart sunk when simply mustering up the words.

"Didn't I tell you not to worry?"

He gazed at me like a husband would a wife. I liked it all too much...his look and the way he handled things, including me.

"Now, grab a plate and dig in."

I bit into the fried chicken breast and almost died. He could cook his ass off. I hated to admit it but I think that moment was the start of me falling for K-Dog.

Not even five minutes into me enjoying my meal, my phone started buzzing. My first thought was to just let it ring. I was exhausted and the last thing I wanted to do was talk. When it continued to ring I looked to see who it was.

"It's about time," I mumbled.

"Hello," I answered semi-pissed. I'd been calling often only to be sent to voicemail.

"Zsaset," she said with a cracked voice.

The tone of her voice told me something wasn't right. "Hey Ma. Where you been? I've been trying to call you."

She was silent.

"Ma!" I yelled. "What's wrong?" I asked, pushing the plate away from me. I could see K-Dog watching me with concern from the corner of my eye.

My mother spoke with a heavy heart. "There was a fire here in my apartment."

"What?" I yelled! I stood up then paced the floor.

I swear it felt like my heart stopped. "Are y'all okay?"

She said yes but I could tell she wasn't.

"Thank God. You scared the crap out of me. What happened?"

"I wasn't feeling well but Ryan was hungry so I tried to make him some oatmeal." She paused. Then hit me with, "Mmph...mmph...ummm. I fell asleep Zsaset and left the oatmeal cooking on the stove. It caught fire," she said, crying so hard I could barely understand what she was saying.

"Ma, calm down. It's okay." I could still hear her choking back her tears when I asked, "Why didn't you tell me you weren't doing well, I would've come home for a few days."

She sighed in exasperation. "I didn't want to bother you."

"Well, why didn't you call Frankie?"

"Baby, your brother is too busy trying to take over the world. He doesn't have time to be driving over here for stuff like that."

So not even the chosen one has time for his ailing mother? He's such a fraud! I thought. I couldn't dare say that to her. She thought he was going to be the next President of the United States.

"Zsaset, that's not the only reason I called." She took a deep breath. "When the kitchen caught fire, the police and fire departments were called and when I told them what happened they called child services."

My entire body froze and I became nauseous immediately.

"Fuck! What did they say?" I said, rushing over to K-Dog's arms.

Of course he consoled me, rubbing my shoulders. Calm down, he mouthed.

"They said I wasn't fit to watch Ryan so they took him. Baby, I'm so sorry."

"Took him where?"

"I don't know. Some foster home, I guess."

My nerves made my heart pound like I had just run a marathon, my stomach felt queasy and I was lightheaded. The next thing you know, I let out a loud cry and I didn't stop for a few minutes. My crying was scaring Zeta so I closed my eyes, inhaled and exhaled, trying to calm down. I kept repeating, "Okay, it's gonna be all right...okay, it's gonna be all right," I said, wiping my eyes. My mother began to speak but I could barely comprehend what she was saying because my whole body had shut down by this time. Hearing me cry made my mother sob as she recited a prayer asking God for help. She cried out, "Jesus, help us! Jesus, help us, Lord!"

I paced around the kitchen in disbelief that this was actually happening.

"This is the day that I will never be able to live down. I'm still having a hard time, even as a believer in Christ and His mercy, to forgive myself. I would give anything to go back and change this one thing," my mother said.

"Ma, it's not your fault. It's mine. I should've brought Ryan here with me. I'm his mother!"

I watched as K-Dog lifted Zeta into his arms and took her into the other room. "Ma, I'm on my way home. I'm going to go get him."

"There's no need, Zsaset. They already said you can't see him."

"What the hell they mean I can't see him? That's my damn son."

"I'm just telling you what the lady said. It wasn't Mrs. Smith, it was a new caseworker. She said you can call tomorrow and she'll let you know what steps you have to take to get him back."

I felt bad about the way I spoke to my mother so I apologized. I know she would've never done anything to put Ryan in harm's way. She loved that little boy like he was her own so for them to take Ryan because of a small kitchen fire infuriated me.

If you ask me, Child Protective Services was just as corrupt as politicians. They would "kid jack" your children for even the smallest mishap. They were really swift in their actions this time. They had the full extent of their powers laid on us and Ryan was removed from my mom's care just like that. Once again, I let my family down. If I would've driven to Norfolk, to check on them this probably would've never happened. Instead, I wasted time on O.B, a man! Right then and there, I made a vow to myself. Getting my son back, and finding a stable living situation was now my top priority.

fourteen...

The morning started off rocky considering my anxiety had gotten the best of me. Between the call from my mom and worrying about being connected to the shooting, I woke up with a major migraine. How could my life spiral out of control in less than twenty-four hours? What had I done to deserve such bad luck? To make matters worse, O.B was up early irritating the shit out of me for meanness.

When I walked into the bathroom to do my hair, I noticed my expensive Sedu flat iron cord cut in several places. Instantly, I hissed a fit. "You petty mothafucka! Leave me the fuck alone!"

"Leave then, bitch!" he shouted from the bottom of the stairs.

With all the rage inside of me, I bolted down the staircase and confronted him. "You think you doing all this childish shit means something to me!"

Little did he know whenever he would do something spiteful or mean to me, I did vindictive little things right back to return the favor. I would scrub the toilet with his toothbrush, blow my nose on his pillow, spit in his food, or flick cigarette ashes into his open bottles of beer. But my biggest revenge hadn't come yet.

He was fucking with the wrong chick.

Before I knew it, he'd yanked the flat iron from my hand, opened the front door, and tossed one of my favorite items into the middle of the street.

"Nigga, those cost $160.00. You're going to replace that shit."

"Why don't you just get the fuck out! Move bitch," he blasted as he shot by me and slammed the front door.

Of course, Zeta was upstairs crying again. That seemed to be the norm. Some days she'd just cry while some nights she had nightmares. After calming her down, I dressed Zeta and explained to her she would be spending the day with Miss Brenda, the lady with the big pool. She was delighted since she was already acquainted with her kids.

Before I could get down the stairs, Zeta was screaming "C'mon, Mommy."

"Zeta, slow your roll, little girl." I grabbed my purse and tried to maintain my composure. She had no idea all of the issues swirling around in my head. I took two more Excedrin Migraine pills and took her next door.

On the way to work, I called the number my mother had given me to check on the status of Ryan. Each time, voicemail.

I tried again.

And again.

And again.

Voicemail.

It pissed me off but I figured I'd try back on my first break.

I called Brina next.

"Hey Boyyyyy! I thought you forgot all about us," she yelled into the phone.

I tried to manage a fake laugh. "Never that. I've just been busy."

"Busy doing what? Riding that dick."

I chuckled. "Girl, please. Now that I'm up here, this nigga acting a damn fool and getting me wrapped up in all kinds of bullshit."

"Oh, fuck that! Are you kiddin' me?"

"Nope, we broke up. But I'm good."

Brina tried to convince me to come back home but my pride wouldn't let me.

After my talk with Brina, I was so emotionally exhausted from trying to figure out what went wrong, I pulled into the parking lot and prayed hard before walking into the mall.

I got to my job within two minutes after hopping out the car. The store was unusually packed for a Wednesday but then I realized it was the first of the month. I clocked in and headed for the sales floor. My day went well except when these ghetto ass chicks tried on about twenty pairs of shoes and only brought one pair. It amazed me how they would get checks for their children but spent it on their hair and nails while the children looked like their hair hadn't been touched by a comb in years.

By two o' clock, and no break, I had done six hundred dollars in sales and was ready for lunch. As I walked to the food court, I prayed to God that there wouldn't be a repeat of yesterday's shooting. Everything was quiet so I looked around to see what I wanted to eat. I felt like some McDonald's fries so I stood in line and waited for my order to be taken. When it was my turn to order, a cute petite white girl took my order. If I were to close my eyes, I'd have sworn I was listening to a sista.

"What's up, girl? Whatcha need?" she asked, sounding like she was straight out of the hood.

I was taken aback because I couldn't believe she was the manager. She just didn't strike me as management material. After waiting for hot fries to come up she quickly placed my order on a tray and handed it to me.

"Have a good day, girlfriend."

"You too," I said with a puzzled look on my face.

Girlfriend? Bitch please, you have no idea what it's like to walk a day in my shoes. Maybe she thought it was cool to act black. Maybe she wanted to be under investigation. She had no idea what troubles came with being me at the moment.

I grabbed my tray and walked over to the tables. It took

me a while to find somewhere to sit because most of the tables were dirty. It amazed me how the first of the month brought all the bad ass kids and their mommas to the mall. One of those little suckers almost knocked my food out of my hands. I had to find a seat quick. As I looked around, I heard a familiar voice trying to get my attention. I turned and saw it was the manager from McDonald's. Nodding my head, I gave her the okay. Damn, what did she do, sprint out here?

"Thank you," I said, sliding my tray on the table. It was awkward at first. She just stood there looking at me until she invited herself into the seat across from me. We sat there quietly for what seemed like a half hour.

"My name is Cindy," she said, breaking the silence. "What's yours?"

"It's Zsaset."

"So, how long have you been working here?" she asked.

"It's only my second day," I replied, after taking a sip of my drink.

"Oh, I've been here for almost two years. I like it but it doesn't leave me much of a social life."

I didn't recall asking Cindy anything. Besides, I'd planned on spending my lunch trying to locate Ryan, and finding out how to get him back. Being rude wasn't the best idea, but I needed to get away from Cindy.

As Cindy kept rambling, I noticed a guy sitting near us staring me. He wasn't your average looking guy. He had some type of African tribal scar that covered the whole right side of his face. His eyes were blood shot red like he had been up for days and his clothes were two sizes too big. I had never seen him before and his glares weren't those of someone who was maybe interested in me. It was like he was looking through me. I was getting a little uncomfortable so I decided to leave. *Damn, is he an undercover cop?* I thought.

"Well, gotta get back to work," I stated, then stood up.

"Okay, maybe we can do this again if it's all right with you of course."

"Sure." I shot her the best smile available under the circumstances. That was a random encounter.

I took one last sip of my Dr. Pepper then grabbed my tray and emptied it. As I walked back to the store, I couldn't help but think how I'd misjudged Cindy. She was actually cool and probably a good person to hang out with sometime.

When I returned to the store, Vicki's expression warned me that something was wrong. I paused and allowed a deep breath to escape. I couldn't handle much more.

"Someone's here to see you, Zsaset?"

"Who?" I blasted.

"It's a man in a suit. He claims he's a detective." She shrugged her shoulders. "He's in the back stockroom waiting on you."

"A detective?" I asked, feeling totally faint.

"Yep!"

I started pacing back and forth. I assumed it was about the murders in Mosby. It seemed as if I couldn't wrap my head around how to act, or what to say before I walked to the back. If I said I wasn't there I was fucked. If I said I was at the apartment I was fucked. I took several deep breaths then walked towards the back room.

As soon as I saw the detectives' round, chubby face my heart started pounding. He was heavy-set white man with very little facial hair, or hair on top of his head. Sporting a pair of Oakley sunshades, he removed them and showed me his badge.

"Hi. I'm Detective Berry. You mind if we talk for a minute?"

"Sure."

He didn't want to talk in front of everyone so he asked me to walk outside the store with him. We sat at a bench a few feet away from the store and my noisy ass co-workers.

"What's this about?" I asked.

"Well, it's been brought to our attention that you may have some information about the shootings of Freddie Hyman and Darrell McKnight," he said, pulling out his notebook and pen.

"I don't know how that's possible. I'm not familiar with either of those names. When and where did this even take place?"

"In the Mosby Court projects."

"Oh, I know where that is?"

"Yes, I'm sure," he said mockingly. "Whose place did you visit?"

"No one. Just rode through there with a friend."

"Would this be the drug dealing friends that you're staying with?"

My eyes damn near popped out of my head. As chills shot through my body, "I said firmly, "I know nothing about any drugs, Sir."

"Oh," he laughed, and patted his sweaty forehead with a handkerchief. "That's right, and you don't have any information about the shooting on Mosby Court around the time when you were riding through, either, right?"

"No. I'm sorry, I don't. Are you sure you have the right person? I'm not even from this area."

"I know exactly where you're from," he spat, showing me that he wasn't playing any games. "Do you know Coley Rounds or Lina Hollister?"

I had to think carefully how to answer his question. If I said yes, then that would put me at the scene of the crime. If I said no but someone saw me there, he would know I was hiding something. Fuck, what do I do?

"I think I met them once but it was when I first moved to Richmond."

"Do you remember where you were when you met them?"

"No, I'm not too familiar with this area yet?" I said, shaking my head.

"Zsaset, look it's in your best interest to be honest with me here."

"I am being honest with you. I don't know those guys, and I had absolutely nothing to do with them getting hurt."

I almost said murder which would have really given my ass up since he only told me that there was a shooting. I was sure he knew I was lying because he stared at me for long time before asking me the next question.

"What if I told you Lina Hollister said you were in her apartment the night those fellas were murdered? And I do mean murdered," he stated firmly, with his voice on high.

I sat as calmly as possible with direct eye contact while the detective grilled me. When he saw he wasn't getting any-where with me he handed me his card, and told me to give with him a call if I remembered anything. I took the card and shook his hand firmly, then exhaled the moment he turned to walk away. When I got back to the store, I ran into the stock room, sweating from every pore of my body. Hurriedly, I fell to my knees in search for my purse and anxiety meds, which no longer worked on my ever increasing stressful life. I had a feeling it was only a matter of time before I was sitting in a jail cell. No-body could know about this. I had to do my best to keep a straight face, although I could not hide the sweat on my brow. I would have to worry silently.

At 4:00 p.m., the closing crew came in and that's when the drama began. I could not take much more. Vicki intro-duced me to two female employees. Londa, the slim, dark-skinned, medium height one didn't seem very friendly. The other one, Michelle was a little overweight, light skinned and very quiet. Londa was lazy and loud as hell. She just stood around acting stank while I helped all the customers. That was no problem since we worked on commission, it just meant more money for me.

A couple of times I caught her cutting her eyes at me. This bitch did not really want it with me right now. I was going to step to her but I felt kind of sorry for her. Nobody in the store liked her. I don't think she even liked herself. Not only was she rude to us, she was rude to the customers. I didn't give a damn what she was going through since my life seemed to be falling apart before my eyes. If she didn't want to get slapped, she had better readjust her attitude towards me.

"Vicki, what's Londa's deal?" I asked as we were both clocking out.

"Oh, don't pay her any attention. She has issues."

"So, what? I got issues, too. All I know is she's gonna get a busted lip if she don't stop gritting on me."

Vicki just shook her head and laughed as I left the store.

As soon as I got in the car I called the number to Child Services again. It seemed to be the direct line of the woman who'd taken Ryan and given my mother her card. After not being able to reach her, I tried my mom's number. No answer from her either. I blew my breath loudly as I did ninety miles per hour all the way to get Zeta.

Walking into the house and seeing O.B made me want to go back to work and pull a double shift. He was his usual cold self. He even called a girl and held a very intimate conversation with her on the phone to get a rise out of me. I tried to ignore his stupidity, but it was impossible not to get upset. I wanted to kick his ass in the head until he was dead. That was when I realized that I needed to get the hell out of their place, fast. My day-dreaming was interrupted. "What you doing?" K- Dog asked, as he walked into the kitchen.

"I'm just thinking."

"Thinking about what? Let me guess, O.B, right?"

"Not really. I'm thinking about how nice it would be to have my own place."

"Zsaset, you have to stop lettin' that nigga get to you like this."

"I know, but it's hard. As soon as I get enough money I'm outta here."

"Well, if you need any help just let me know," he said.

Well, I may need more than that," I told him, looking deeply into his eyes. That's when I broke down and told him about my visit from Detective Berry.

fifteen...

The next day proved to be a real test of my strength. I hadn't slept at all the night before. Not only did I have to deal with wondering if I was going to be arrested for the shooting, I had to deal with my guilt related to my son, Ryan. I'd beat myself up thinking about how my many mistakes led to him being away from his family. It took everything in me not to call out of work but if I was going to be moving into my own spot, I had to keep my job so I go prepared for work despite my lack of sleep.

As I got ready, my hands wouldn't stop shaking. Every little noise I heard I thought it was the police coming for me. Paranoia had set in. By the time I got to work, I was in a bad mood and Londa staring at me made me even angrier.

"Why are you staring at me?" I asked with an attitude.

"I'm not staring at you," she said.

"Yes, you are. If there's a problem, let's solve it right now so I can get on with my day," I said sharply.

She was so shocked she didn't even respond. As a matter of fact, she was on her best behavior for the rest of the day. She wasn't a bad person at all. She just needed someone to put her in her place, and I was the right one for the job.

Around five o'clock our assistant manager told me to clock out for dinner. As I stood in front of McDonald's trying to decide what I wanted, Cindy motioned for me to get in her line. Smiling, she handed me a tray with a Big Mac, fries and a Dr.

I Shoulda' SEEN HIM Coming

Pepper drink. *Damn, she remembered what I ordered yesterday,* I thought to myself. That was nice.

After finding a corner table to sit at, I pulled out my phone to call my mother.

"Hello," my mom answered quietly.

"Hey, I was calling to see if you've heard anything from Child Services."

"No, I haven't. Did you call them?"

"Yeah, I've been calling since yesterday but no one is picking up. I've left like ten damn messages."

"Well, maybe someone will get back to you before they close."

"They're already closed, Ma. It's 5:15."

"I don't know what to tell you, baby."

"Don't worry about it. I know what to do. I'll just keep calling until someone answers the phone. If they don't answer by the time I get off, I'm coming to Norfolk tomorrow. I gotta get my son!"

I told my mother I would keep her posted and hung up the phone. I sat motionless. I didn't even touch my food. Everything was coming down on me at the same time and for the first time in my life, I didn't know what to do.

My appetite was next to none, but while I picked at my food, Londa showed up at the table and apologized for the way she'd been acting. I certainly didn't need any extra beefs so I accepted her apology. I found out that Londa and I had some things in common. We were both dealing with lunatics at home. I had O.B and she had her mother. She told me that her mother was schizo. Her mom thinks she's an FBI agent. Londa said her mother carries five loaded guns on her every day. She swears someone's after her. She even pulled a gun on Londa one day saying, "I know you trying to kill me."

I was like, "Damn!" I saw why she was so stressed. It turned out she wasn't as bad I thought. In fact, she had some jokes that lightened my mood for like thirty seconds.

Just as we were about to leave, Cindy interrupted us. "So

what's up girl?" she asked, standing over me.

"Nothing much," I said, pulling out a chair for her. "This is my co-worker, Londa."

They exchanged greetings as Cindy sat down at the table. "Your assistant manager mentioned you were looking for a place," Cindy said.

"Yeah, why you know somewhere?"

"There are some apartments not far from here that are reasonable," she said, as she wrote down the address. "You should look into it."

"If you need a roommate, look me up."

"Okay. I'll do that."

Londa and I dumped our trash, left the food court and headed back to work.

I headed to the front of the store after I clocked back in and secured my purse in Larry's desk. While I was straightening the shoe wall, a nice looking gentleman with a limp walked in. He was 6'3 with big hazel eyes and dreads. Iced out with diamonds, he wore a Fendi sweater and jeans. *Damn he's fine*, I thought as I rushed over to greet him.

"Can I help you find something today?" I said, flirting.

"No," he snapped.

What the hell is his problem? I thought. He strolled over to the children's section and picked up two styles of Nike sneakers.

"Get me deez in a 13 1/2, and don't take all day," he said in a nasty tone.

"Oh, now you need help?" I said sarcastically.

He didn't find me amusing and even looked me up and down before sitting down on the bench in the middle of our sales floor.

I gripped the shoes, and switched to the stockroom. As I walked back out onto the floor, I noticed his eyes widening. "Yo... hurry up. I got shit to do!" he yelled.

"Excuse me?" I asked, bobbing my head.

"You heard me. Hurry up."

"Look, I don't appreciate you talking to me like that."

"Do I look like I give a fuck about what you do or don't appreciate? Just ring my shit up," he said, throwing the money at me.

Londa knew I was about to let his ass have it, so she quickly walked up to the register and took over the sale. As she handed him his bags, he gave me one last glare and left.

"Zsaset, do you know who that was," Londa said.

"No, and I don't care. Don't nobody talk to me like that."

"Girl…that was Dolo. He's the biggest and most dangerous drug dealer in Richmond. He has murdered people for looking at him wrong."

"Oh well, he'll get over it," I said as if I didn't care.

"I don't know how guys are where you're from, but here they kill girls just as quick as they kill guys around here. They don't care about nothing or no one. Just watch yourself," she said.

When I got home that night, I quickly showered and got in the bed. Unfortunately, I couldn't get to sleep. I tossed and turned all that night. With all of the problems I had going on, why was Dolo on my mind? The cold look in his eyes haunted me, so I just stared at the ceiling. That is, until my thoughts were interrupted. My phone started to ring loudly. When I looked at the number, my palms began to sweat.

"Hello, may I speak to Mrs. Jones," the woman asked.

"This is she," I replied.

"Mrs. Jones, this is Mrs. Smith from Child Protective Services. I'm in the office working late so I wanted to touch base with you about your son."

"I thought someone else was working on my case."

"Yes, that would be one of my coworkers, but she's out on medical leave so I'm taking over some of her cases. Your case happens to be one of them; a priority, as a matter of fact."

I felt like my air was about to be cut off. Her voice was so stern and business like. I thought for sure she was going to give me bad news.

"Okay, I need to put you on speaker because I'm trying to do a million things at the same time."

"That's fine," I said, as I sat up in the bed.

I heard the phone being placed on the receiver, then she started to speak.

"First of all, I told you before that if there were any further incidents with Ryan I would be placing him in foster care. Now, we have this fire incident at your mother's residence."

"Yes ma'am, I know."

"As you can imagine, things could've been worse and with your mother's medical conditions, we felt it best to place Ryan in foster care."

I was just about to ask her where he was when she started to speak again.

"Now, he is only with this family temporarily until our investigation is complete. Since you live in Richmond, we will pair you up with a social worker there who will be a liaison between you and our office. They will primarily be visiting your home randomly to make sure you have established a safe and stable home environment for him. If you haven't then he will be placed permanently with a family."

"Can I see him?" I asked nervously.

"Yes, I'll call you in about a week or so and let you know where and when."

"Okay, thank you so much."

"Don't thank me just yet. It's not a done deal until I file some paperwork."

I felt a little better after our conversation ended. But I still had this gnawing at the pit of my stomach that said things were about to get worse before they got better. My conscience was beginning to get the best of me. For so long, I didn't have one and now I was starting to see what really mattered; me and my children.

I Shoulda' SEEN HIM Coming

 *sixteen...*

Casually dressed, I set out to find an apartment. I had to find a place close to K-Dog's house, so I could keep Brenda as my babysitter. Zeta was already comfortable with her and I didn't want her to have get use to someone new.

I drove maybe two miles before I lucked up on some apartments that looked fairly new. I walked into the rental office and inquired about a two-bedroom. To my surprise, the complex was running a special.

Still half asleep, I filled out the application and paid the thirty dollar application fee. The rental agent said she would get back to me in three days. Before leaving, I turned towards the lady and asked her how soon I could move in if I got approved.

"You can move in as soon as you want. I already have some apartments ready."

That was all I needed to hear. For the rest of the day, I just kept imagining myself in my own place. Being in the house with

O.B was like serving a life sentence in prison. He made my life miserable. I just wanted to be free and clear of him once and for all. This would prove to be easier said than done.

• • •

During the next two days, I was on pins and needles. I

couldn't eat or sleep. Every few minutes I found myself checking my voicemail. It was day three and I still hadn't heard from the rental agent. And that worried me. She finally called that evening with crushing news that I needed a co-signer since I hadn't been employed for six months yet. I was devastated. Now what was I going to do? I had no choice but to find someone. Then it hit me. Cindy was looking for a place, too. I called McDonald's and asked to speak with her. She got on the phone and I explained what happened and asked if she would be my roommate. Without hesitation, she agreed. "I'll go fill out the application tomorrow," she said.

The next day at work, I was so nervous I couldn't concentrate. I figured if I prayed hard enough, God would get tired of me whining and grant my wish. Sure enough, he heard me. I knew it when Cindy came bursting into the store screaming.

"We got it. We can move in next Saturday," she said, jumping up and down.

"Thank God," I said, throwing my hands up in the air.

"Well, I have to get back to work. I'll talk to you later, roomie. Let's go out and celebrate tomorrow, Zsaset. We deserve it."

"What?" Vicki and Londa said in unison. They wondered what all the hype was about.

"Me and Cindy got an apartment together. She wants to go to a club Saturday to celebrate, but I don't know." I developed a solemn look all too quickly. "With so many problems hanging over my head, I need to just stay home and chill with Zeta."

"Nonsense. We're all going. Count us in," Londa said.

"If you guys insist," I stated, prancing around the store. Somehow I felt like going out would be a big mistake.

When it was closing time, Vicki pulled me to the side.

"Please don't take this the wrong way, but don't you think you're moving a little too fast with Cindy. I mean, what do you know about her?"

"I know she's a nice girl, she has a job and she can pay

her half of the bills. What else do I need to know?"

"I don't know. It's just something about her. I mean out of everyone that eats at McDonald's why did she latch on to you so fast."

"Maybe it's because I'm that bitch," I said laughing. "Now shut up and let's get the hell up out of this camp."

Everyone was sitting in the living room when I came home that night.

"Hey! Listen up," I said. "I have something to tell y'all." O.B huffed and rolled his eyes, of course. Everyone else just looked at me in anticipation of my news. "It's been real, but I'm moving out next Saturday."

It was a bittersweet moment. Quan and K-Dog were happy for me but sad at the same time. Of course, O.B didn't give a damn. He gave me a devilish grin. I was determined to wipe it off his face. Now was not the time, but I made a mental note to get his ass later.

Although these dudes were like the brothers I never had, Quan was becoming more like a father-figure to me. He was always checking up on me and Zeta, dishing out unwanted advice and throwing me a little pocket money here and there to save for a rainy day. In such a short amount of time, they became family and sort of adopted me and Zeta.

I needed to call Brina to give her a few updates.

As soon as Brina said, "Hello", I started screaming, "Yaaaayyyyy! I got an apartment today."

"OMG, I can't believe you're really doing what you said you were going to do?"

"Excuse me?"

"I didn't mean it like that. I was really worried about you leaving but everything seems to be going okay."

"Not really. I'm still in this mess here. This shit just does not stop and now I'm worried about it all coming back to bite me in the ass. Then there's O.B. He acts like I did something fucked up to him when it was the other way around. A month ago you loved me to death and now you hate me. It doesn't make sense."

"Girl, I stopped trying to make sense of how men act a long time ago. It's a waste of time. I don't even think they know why they act the way they do."

"I just think there's more to his breaking up with me then he's telling me."

"Why the hell are you worried about that nigga? You got your new place…you got a job…start doing you. Fuck him!"

I knew Brina was right. We always promised one another that we would be the kind of friends who tell each other what we need to hear…not what we want to hear. However, I could not waste any more time talking to Brina. She wasn't in Richmond with me and some things I would have to deal with on my own.

• • •

I pulled up in front of Vicki's building and blew the horn. I was anxious to celebrate our getting the new apartment. Londa and Cindy were going to meet us at the club, a place called Aqua. I really had no business celebrating since my son was not with me. I was actually beginning to feel embarrassed for not keeping my family together and even more ashamed that I was not the mother I could have been.

Vicki waved at me from her patio after a few seconds. I rolled down my window and asked if she was ready. She shook her head yes and said she was on her way down.

As soon as Vicki came out of her building, I scoped her from head to toe. *Oh hell no,* I thought to myself. She is not going out with me looking like that. Here I was dressed sharp as a knife with my black Vince Camuto jumper and black platform shoes and this bitch had on a polo shirt and some jeans.

"Vicki, please tell me you're not wearing that to the club," I said, as I did a double take.

"Why? Everyone dresses like dis," she replied, as she jumped in.

"What?" I said, getting a headache. "And it's not dis, it's

this with a "th"."

"Oh, shut up and let me see what you got on, Zsaset," she said, turning on the overhead light.

"You look like a hooker."

"Well, at least I look like a well-paid hooker," I said, as I snapped my fingers.

She laughed. "Let's go, crazy."

We got on 95 and headed downtown to Shockoe Bottom. Londa and Cindy were waiting in the dimly lit parking lot when we arrived.

"Zsaset, girl, what do you have on? That outfit is hot," Cindy said, stepping back to get a better look.

"Finally, someone with a little fashion sense around here. I mean it took a white girl to see what this bitch here couldn't see. Shameless...just shameless." I said, eyeing Vicki.

"I didn't say I didn't like it. I just said you look like a hooker in it, that's all," Vicki said.

"Put down the Hatorade and take some notes!" I screamed, walking towards the door.

I was a bit too much for them because when we got inside,
everyone was staring at me like I was a masterpiece at an art museum. That's right bitches...there's a new boss chick in town.

As we made our way through the crowd, the stares became more evident. I didn't mind, though, because I was there for one reason and one reason only...to get a man.

After a couple of drinks, we were all on the dance floor. I was having the time of my life. It had been a long time since I had been out and I felt the weight lifting off my shoulders. I didn't even allow myself to think about how messed up my life was. I just focused on moving into my new apartment and moving on without O.B. I would have to keep in touch with K-Dog and Quan and stop by when I dropped off Zeta. They had been nothing but good to me.

My girls and I were ripping up the dance floor. Four songs in though, I was so exhausted. I sat down and ordered a drink at the bar. Turning around in the chair to check out the prospects, I spotted a familiar face. I couldn't place where I had seen him until he glanced at me with his chilling eyes. Oh my God. I was so shaken I almost spilled my drink. I quickly left the bar, and went to the dance floor to see if I could find Londa. I searched the whole dance floor for her but came up short.

"What's up, girl?" I felt someone grab me by the arm. "You havin' a good time," Londa said.

"I was until a minute ago."

"Why, what's wrong," she asked. "I think I just saw Dolo."

"You probably did. He comes in here with his crew all the time. Don't worry. He probably won't even remember you. He's not the sharpest knife in the drawer."

"Londa, if that was supposed to make me feel better, it didn't. Most killers aren't very bright or they wouldn't kill people."

I continued to look around to make sure Dolo didn't spot me.

"Oh shit, there he is," I said, covering my face.

Seeing him again reminded me of the horror of our first encounter.

"What's your name, shorty?" he said, standing over me.

His towering height and broad shoulders should've been intimidating but instead it radiated nothing but plain sex appeal. He was finer than he was the day I saw him. However, all of that was overshadowed by that hellacious attitude.

"Did you hear me?" he asked again.

"Jazzy," I answered, snapping out of my thoughts.

"Jazzy, I'm Dolo. I'm quite sure your friends at the store told you all about me."

"What store?" I asked.

"Aren't you the chick from Lady Foot Locker that got smart with me?"

And Londa said he wouldn't remember me. I think she's the one with the loose screws. I knew I was going to have to talk my way out of this situation so I tried to back pedal.

"I wouldn't say I got smart with you, I was just merely stating that you were being very rude to me and I didn't appreciate it. If I offended you in anyway, I'm very sorry."

"That's okay, I usually don't like it when people talk to me that way, but there are always exceptions, especially when they're as beautiful as you are, Jazzy." He puffed his cigar. "Where are you from?"

"I'm from the Virginia Beach area.

"That explains why you talk like a white girl."

"I don't talk like a white girl. It's called using correct English," I said to him with an attitude. In my head, I was calling him an ignorant bastard and wondering why I even bothered talking to his ass but my body was saying if you weren't so fine you would be standing here by yourself mothafucka.

He laughed as if he was saying, whatever, bitch. It was so obvious that our conversation was going nowhere so without hesitation, I told him to excuse me. I didn't even give him a chance to respond.

"Let's go," I said, turning towards Londa.

"Jazzy," Dolo shouted. "How you just gone walk away while we in the middle of a conversation?"

I didn't want a scene because I was too classy for that so I took a deep breath and then turned back around. I took a few steps towards Dolo and said, "My friends are ready."

"Well, can I call you?" At this point, we had a small audience and I didn't want to embarrass him.

"Umm…I guess you can." I quickly wrote down a fake number and turned to leave.

"You better not be playing with me, Jazzy. This number better be good." *Not only is the number wrong, the name is wrong too,* I thought. It probably was not wise for me to do that, but I did it anyway. The last thing I needed was another O.B on my hands.

The club was starting to let out when I finally found Vicki and Cindy.

"Where the hell have y'all been all night?" I said.

"Talking to deez guy's from the north side."

"What the hell is deez? The word is these. Say it with me,
these."

"Zsaset, you always correctin' people like you don't use slang."

"The only time you'll hear me speaking slang is when I'm
mad. Y'all bitches use it all day, every day. Notice how I just
said y'all. It's because I'm mad right now. I'm mad that none of
you know how to speak correctly," I said, laughing.

They were pretty pissed at me so they all walked off. I
know the truth hurts, but damn!

Walking towards the car, Cindy dug around in the bottom
of her purse and pulled out her cell phone.

"Who you calling this time of night," I asked.

"None of your business."

"It must be a booty call," I insisted.

"That's right, it's a booty call. It's my new man. You'll
meet him soon. He's gonna help us move in."

I was dying to know if he was white or black, so I asked.
When she said he was black it didn't surprise me, considering
she acted like she was black herself. Waiting for her to finish up
with her call, I watched as Vicki and Londa yelled at guys driving hot cars, trying to get them to pull over. I couldn't believe
how ghetto they were acting. They both could've made the
worst dressed list, not to mention, they weren't very attractive.
They gave a whole new meaning to the phrase beauty is in the
eye of the beholder. Why some whack ass dudes hadn't snatched
those two up was beyond me.

Cindy was on the phone maybe five minutes when I
heard a commotion near the club. I saw a crowd of guys fighting
in the street. It looked like the L.A. riots. I witnessed a guy bust
another guy in the head with a beer bottle. I tried to get my girls'
attention, but they were all preoccupied with men.

I bent over to secure my ankle strap when I heard a loud car engine. I looked up and saw a figure coming in my direction. I then turned side-ways for a better view and a bright-orange, old-ass Maxima slowly drove by. As it did, shots rang out and the crowd began to scatter. I couldn't believe it, but this guy was actually shooting right next to me. The thugs in the car shot back. I heard girls screaming in fear.

Too afraid to move, I dropped to the ground and shielded my body with my arms. It happened so fast, I didn't have time to concern myself with where my girls were. The shooting seemed like it was never going to end. When the shooting was over, two bloody bodies laid on the ground beside me. I couldn't tell if they were dead, but it appeared if they weren't, they would be soon.

When I got up, I stepped around the bodies and took off like a bat out of hell. I headed straight for my car. I heard the sound of sirens growing closer as I fumbled for my keys. I shook like I had Parkinson's disease. The key would not fit in the hole.

Scared and confused, I sat in my car choking down a cig-arette. I was relieved when I saw my girls running up to the car.

"Girl, are you all right," they asked.

"I think so," I said, lighting up my second smoke. "I was so scared something happened to y'all. Who was that guy shoot-ing at people?" I asked.

"Girl, that was Dolo," Vicki said trembling.

"What," I said blown away. "Let's get the hell out of here. I'm not used to no shit like this."

On the way to Vicki's house, the events replayed in my head. I was so fucked up in the head I thought I was going to need a doctor.

"All I have to say is that was the last time I'm going to that
club. I'm not losing my life because a bunch of gun-happy nig-gas want to declare war on each other," I said.

"Zsaset, I'm with you, girl. That was too close for comfort. Are you sure you're okay? Dolo almost shot you."

"Yeah, but I thought I was gonna die. Who is this Dolo fool anyway? Where is he from?" I said.

"New York and he is dangerous as hell. Besides being the biggest drug dealer in Richmond, he's a cold-blooded killer. Just last month, he walked right up to a guy downtown and shot him in the head in broad daylight. The guy shot him back in the leg. That's why he has a limp."

"So, why isn't that fool in jail?" I asked.

"No one will testify against him. He has Richmond locked down."

For the rest of the ride we sat in silence.

By the time I dropped Vicki off, the sun was coming up and I was heading home. All of the commotion at the club wore me out. I just wanted to get into bed.

I opened the door and found O.B lying on the couch. The television wasn't on and there wasn't any music playing. It was almost as if he was waiting up for me. I shut my bedroom door and as I listened quietly on the other side, I heard him get up and come upstairs.

"Awww, he still cares," I mouthed. Now, it was obvious he was waiting up for me, or so I thought. I guess he was worried.

This was the first time I had been out since our break up. I thought to myself, *maybe I had over-reacted about O.B dumping me because of his wife.* Then I thought, *don't be stupid, Zsaset, this nigga is no good for you. Be over it.*

 seventeen...

The sun blazed through my blinds so brightly I had no choice but to get up. I picked Zeta up from Brenda's then made myself some breakfast.

"Hey, I heard you were at the club last night. Did you see that nigga Dolo, actin' like he was a cowboy shootin' up shit?" Quan asked.

"Yes, but if you don't mind, I don't want to talk about it front of you know who," I said, pointing to Zeta.

"That's right, not in my front of my Zeta Beta," K-Dog said.

Quan stopped right away. He was good at always doing what was right. Besides, the last thing I wanted to do was relive last night, so I cut the conversation short and went upstairs to get back in bed. But not even a couple hours later, the sound of toys banging woke me up. I rolled over and looked at my clock. Still stretched out on the bed, I asked Zeta if Quan and K-Dog had left.

"Nope," she said, jumping up and down on the bed.

Blown.

I continued to lay in the bed as I scrolled down my Facebook page. I posted a new status update that read, ***Things have to get better. Tired of all the drama in my life***. I laid my phone down and turned on my side. Minutes later, my phone started to ring. It was a private number but I answered it anyway.

"Hello."

"Hi Mommy," the little voice said.

"Ryan, oh my God. How are you, baby?"

I could barely hear him with all of the noise Zeta was making. "Mommy, I want to talk to Ryan!" she screamed.

"Zeta, wait one second, okay."

She started to pout.

"Ryan, I miss you."

"I miss you, too," he said, emotionless.

Well damn, I thought to myself.

"Why do you sound like that? Are they being nice to you?"

"Yes."

"I know you want to come home, sweetie. I'm working on it."

I didn't know what to think. He was barely talking to me. Every question I asked him, he would answer with one word, but when he finally talked to Zeta he was his normal self. After we talked for a while, there was silence.

"Ryan…Ryan!" I yelled.

There was no answer.

"Hello."

"Hello," a faint female voice sounded.

"Hi, what happened to my son?"

"I don't know he just handed me the phone. I guess he was finished talking," she informed me. The woman who was Ryan's temporary foster mother gave me an update on Ryan, then told me she would have him call me again when he was up to it.

When he felt up to it. What the hell did she mean by that? I started to go off on her ass but I didn't want to make matters worse so I just left it alone.

"Thank you," I told her then slammed the damn phone down.

I was a feeling really down that Ryan didn't want to talk

to me but I tried to remain positive that once we were all together things would be back to normal.

Seeing all the boxes on the floor made me realize we were actually moving in a week, so I tried to divert my attention to keep from thinking about Ryan. I pulled out my book and started to jot down notes for my move. I called Cindy to discuss how we would split the bills, but we decided to hammer it out over dinner instead of on the phone.

That evening, I met Cindy at Cheesecake Factory.

"Cindy, this is my daughter, Zeta."

"Oh, she is so cute," she said, giving her a hug.

"Thank you. You guys should get along really well. I've been blessed to have an angel for a daughter," I said proudly.

We looked over the menus until the waitress came to take our order. Zeta wanted to start with desert but I convinced her to eat some food first. When the tired looking waitress finally wobbled over to our table, we placed our orders. I ordered the Chicken Fettuccine for myself and Zeta. Cindy ordered the Cajun Jambalaya Pasta.

"I can't wait to move in," Cindy said.

"Yeah, I know girl. My ex is driving me crazy."

"So, what happened with you guys?"

"To make a long story short, he made me believe there was a future for us. But now that he got the goodies, he's through with me."

"That's a man for you. Don't let him get you down. Trust me, I've had my share of dummies too, but I think I've found true love this time."

Hearing Cindy saying she found true love gave me hope that I would find a man to really love me one day.

Before we were even finished going over everything, Zeta was falling out of her chair. Her crawling on the floor took the cake.

"She's getting restless. I better get her home," I said to Cindy.

I told her I would see her tomorrow. It must have been

I Shoulda' SEEN HIM Coming

the cheesecake Zeta ate because she was wired. As I pulled out
of the parking lot, a song by Drake was on the radio. Zeta tried
to keep up but was no match for me. I loved me some Drake.

"What's the move? Can I tell truth?
If I was doing this for you
Then I have nothing left to prove, nah
This for me, though
I'm just tryna stay alive and take care of my people
And they don't have no award for that
Trophies, trophies

I turned to my baby and frowned. I knew my baby girl
was too hip for her age. She knew plenty of rap lyrics but no
nursery rhymes. She could do all the video dances, but she
didn't know the hokey pokey. In the back of my mind, I knew it
was because of my lifestyle.

I was a quarter of a mile from K-Dog's house when I noticed a cream colored Infiniti speeding up on my tail. I couldn't
make out the driver's face, but it was clear they wanted me. My
heart raced more and more as I sped, pressing the gas harder and
harder. Finally, I could see that it was a woman. That had my
mind going crazy.

Who was it?

And what did she want?

After a few seconds of running up on me like she was
going to hit me, the driver eased up on the gas. I started to pull
over but I was too scared. My main concern was getting Zeta
into the house quickly so I sped down the street changing lanes
to try and throw the driver off my trail. She was three cars behind me when I turned onto our street.

When I looked in my rear view mirror again, I noticed
the car was gone. I grabbed my chest and tried to catch my
breath. I pulled in front of the house and jumped out checking
both ends of the street. I was on Zeta's side of the car unbuck-
ling her from her car seat when I heard the loud screeching of
tires. Instantly, I panicked when the same cream colored Infiniti
screeched to a stop in front of us. I looked up and couldn't be-

lieve my eyes.

Why the fuck was she here? I thought she was in New York.

It was crazy-ass Yaya.

"Bitch, I see you still here. Didn't I tell yo' ass to leave my man's house?" Yaya screamed through her car window, with spit flying out of her mouth.

Quickly, I yanked Zeta out of the car, pulling her close to my chest, and jetted up the sidewalk towards the front door.

"Yeah bitch, you better be scared cause I got sumthin' for you!" she yelled, racing the engine like a race car driver ready for take off.

When I realized Yaya wasn't going to get out of the car, I got bold and taunted her.

"This is not your man's house, bitch," I yelled back, standing on the porch.

"Oh, you getting buck? Listen tramp, he will never be yours. He's my fuckin' husband and if you know what's good for that ass you'll get the fuck away from him," she said, with her long colorful nail moving swiftly, and pointed at me.

"Fuck you!" I spat.

Pissed, Yaya sped off leaving a trail of black tire marks behind.

That bitch is crazy! I thought.

As soon as I walked in and locked the door, I ran over to the window to make sure she was really gone.

"What the hell is wrong with you?" O.B asked.

"Your crazy ass wife was out there," I told him, laying Zeta on the couch.

O.B stomped over to the door, opened it and looked out.

"Why you always gotta play fuckin' games? She ain't out there."

I walked up behind him and peered over his shoulder.

"I'm telling you. She was just out there yelling and screaming at me like a mad woman."

"Yep, she was," Zeta chimed in.

"Zeta, stay outta grown folks business," I told her.

With his face turned up O.B said, "You'll do anythin' to get my attention, won't you?"

"Fuck you! Ain't nobody checking for your dumb ass," I roared, as I ran up to my room.

A few minutes later, I heard footsteps stomping up the stairs. I was hoping it was K-Dog because I was so over arguing with O.B. I held my breath as I slowly turned around.

This mothafucka don't have anything else to do but fuck with me.

"Hey, I need to talk to you, while Zeta's downstairs," O.B said like something was killing him.

"Why is it when it comes to me you can get all rowdy, but you allow Yaya to punk you like a little bitch?"

My hands were on my hips and my facial expression proved that I was tired of his shit.

O.B sat on my bed with this stupid look on his face. He kept shaking his head back and forth like something was really bothering him.

"What is it? Spit it out! What do you need to tell me?"

"She's blackmailing me," he said reluctantly.

"What? How is she blackmailing you?"

Sighing and turning his head away in shame, he rubbed his head. "I did something stupid about 3 years ago."

"And what's that?" I softened my tone a bit, hoping he'd tell me.

"It's bad."

"Well, how does she know about it?"

"She was there."

"Okay, well, that makes her an accessory to the crime, right? So, she's not really gonna tell on you because she would have to admit her part in it."

O.B dropped his head again. "That's not all, Zsaset. She knows about the Mosby shooting too."

My stomach felt queasy hearing those words. I sat beside

him worriedly, and made him look at me. How does she know? And are you saying she knows I did it?" My voice trembled.

"I haven't figured that out yet."

My nerves were doing flips. I stood up, pulled a Newport out of the box that was sitting on my dresser and lit it. "So, what you're telling me is…we're fucked. This bitch has you by the balls and there's nothing you can do about it."

"Zsaset, you don't understand. I did something so unforgivable that if anyone found out, not only would I go to jail, I would be a marked man in jail. I probably wouldn't even make it through the night."

"Well, whatever it is, you've got to do something about her," I said, pissed that he'd gotten me into this predicament.

"If it wasn't for my son, I would've been killed Yaya."

"Where is he?"

O.B's voice sunk when he started to speak of his son. He hadn't seen him in a year because Yaya sent him to go stay with some relatives and O.B didn't know where they lived.

"This is why I got this," he said, pointing to the QT tattoo on his face. "His name is Quentin Terrell. It's a reminder that he's always with me."

A part of me wanted to hold him in my arms. The other part of me wanted to strangle him. He couldn't kill the bitch, but there was nothing stopping me from killing her ass.

I Shoulda' SEEN HIM Coming

eighteen...

Several days later, move-in day came. Hallelujah! Cindy didn't have much except clothes and personal items to move in, while me on the other hand, had a few deliveries from pieces of furniture that I'd purchased, compliments of K-Dog. Although it only took us two hours to move in, we sweated like slaves. I plopped on one of the boxes and drank an ice-cold beer after the first sign that we were done. I couldn't believe it. I was finally here, in my new apartment.

The split-level, roommate style had its benefits. Our rooms were on opposite ends of the apartment. That was perfect because I didn't want to hear her getting busy. I'm glad we each had our own bathrooms. I always got petty about my bathroom.

There was a large kitchen, a large den that could be used as a spare bedroom, a small courtyard in the front for Zeta to play in, and a swimming pool was only steps away from our door. I could finally breathe again.

My thoughts were interrupted by a knock at the door. I opened it and to my surprise it was the last person in the world I expected to see.

"What the hell are you doing here?" I said taken aback.

"Taking care of business. Why you here?" he said. O.B paused for a moment and then said, "Wait a minute, this isn't your new place, is it?"

"What the hell you think?" I stood there, debating my

next move. Just as I was about to close the door, Cindy came running down the steps.

O.B looked over and saw her and then grabbed me and whispered in my ear, "Please play along."

I was squirming and trying to wiggle out of his embrace. "Hey, I assume you two know one another," Cindy said.

"Yeah, this is my sister. You didn't tell me you were rooming with my sister."

"Your sister? I didn't know you had a sister."

He doesn't, I thought to myself.

"I thought you just had brothers." She stood there confused and a little suspicious. O.B sensed her distrust and continued with his performance.

"Zsaset, you talked to Ma? What's she been doing?"

I stumbled over my words. "Ah, ah, yeah, I mean no I haven't talked to her in a long time."

My insides fumed while O.B had a big ass grin on his face. "Yeah, well you know you better call her. You know how she gets."

I still couldn't believe it. Cindy was actually dating O.B. In shock, I stood there motionless. I felt like I was in the Twilight Zone or being Punk'D or something.

Cindy interrupted, "O.B, come on in and chat with your sister. I have to run to the store for some hangers." She plastered a big wet kiss on his lips on her way out, while glancing back at us both. I wasn't sure she was buying it.

As soon as the door shut, I looked at O.B. "Why in the hell did you tell her I was your sister?"

I shot him a nasty stare.

"I didn't know what else to say."

"How about the truth?" I threw the closest thing to me in his direction; a roll of paper towels.

"I couldn't, Zsaset. Look, it's clear me and you are done. You know I'ma be bangin' somebody, that's what men do. I just happened to meet Cindy when I was leaving the mall one day, and the rest is history. Just please do not fuck this up. She gives

really good medusa, too," O.B. laughed. "Even better than you."
That shit wasn't the least bit funny.

I crossed my arms and asked, "So, why not tell her the
truth now?"

"I don't want to hurt her," he fired.

"Un-fuckin-believable! You son of a bitch. You didn't
have a problem hurting me, but you have a problem hurting
her." Why did I let this stupid mothafucka exert this amount of
control over me? I asked myself.

"Look, I cared about you, Zsaset, but my wife won't
stand by and watch the two of us together."

"Oh, and she's fine with you fuckin' a white girl?"

He stood there for a few minutes.

"So, are you goin' to tell Cindy we used to date?" he
asked me with pleading eyes.

It took me about thirty seconds to answer. I wanted him
to sweat. "I guess I'll keep your little secret. Let Yaya beat up
on her for a change," I said jokingly.

I could tell he was relieved because he bear hugged me.

"So, I'm your sister, huh?" I asked, smiling and feeling
like I'd been played.

"I guess so."

Not only did he tell her I was his sister, he told her K-
Dog and Quan were his brothers. I went from having one
brother to having four brothers in one day.

"O.B, what am I supposed to do when she starts asking
me questions?"

"Just make up somethin'. You act like you don't know
how to lie. I hear things about you, you're not perfect," he fired.

"I don't lie, thank you."

"Yeah, whatever you say. Tell Cindy I had to make a run
and I'll call her later," he said, walking out the door.

After watching him speed out of the parking lot, I started
unpacking boxes again until Cindy got back from the store.

"You finish unpacking already?" she said from the
kitchen.

"Not yet. I just wanted to take a break before Vicki got here with Zeta."

When the doorbell rang, I thought maybe it was Vicki from work but it was K –Dog.

"I just dropped by to see the new crib," he said, snooping around.

"Boy, I'm glad to see you. Let's talk out here." I pulled him by the hand and led him to the courtyard.

"What's wrong?"

"K-Dog, I can't get rid of this mothafucka to save my life. Guess who my roommate's boyfriend is?"

"Naw," he said, dropping his jaw. "Please don't tell me."

"Yep, my biggest nightmare," I screamed.

I explained the whole twisted story to K-Dog to get his opinion. Shrugging his shoulders, he just rubbed his head as if he didn't have an answer to my question.

"This situation calls for a shrink," he said. "That nigga, O.B is crazy as hell."

"No, if anyone's crazy, it's me. I can't believe I agreed to go along with this dumb shit. I moved to get away from him and now I have to see his ass every day. And with another woman at that. Ain't that a bitch?"

We were still talking when a familiar car pulled up. I almost cried when I saw her face. "If ever I needed you, I need you now, chica!" I screeched, as I gave her a big bear hug.

"Boy, what's wrong?" Brina asked, while smiling at K-Dog.

"I'll tell you all about it in a few. Looks like I'm not the only one you came to see," I said, raising my eyebrows.

She smiled but K-Dog kept looking through his phone like he was looking for the call she should've made before she showed up.

He said, "Hi" and gave her a hug but he didn't seem happy to see her. I didn't even want to begin to try and figure them out. I had my own problems so I was just going to stay out of it.

K-Dog told us he needed to go handle some business then disappeared quickly into my apartment.

"What the hell was that?" I asked.

"I don't know. I think he's seeing someone," she said, rubbing her hands through her newly relaxed hair.

"I haven't seen him with anyone so I doubt it."

"Well...something is off with him," she said, getting an instant attitude.

"Speaking of things being off. Have you talked to Nicole? Every time I call her she sends me to voicemail."

"Naw, I haven't talked to her or seen her in awhile. She's not answering my calls either," Brina said, with a nosy look on her face. "I wonder what the hell she's up to."

"I don't know, but it can't be good since she's ignoring us," I said, laughing.

As we talked, I noticed a Crown Vic, better known as a detective's work vehicle, ride through slowly like he was looking for someone. When he pulled his shades down, my blood pressure rose and almost caused me to pass out.

"Zsaset, what's wrong?" she asked, holding me up.

"It was Detective Berry. The one who keeps calling and questioning me."

If I was part of an ongoing investigation I couldn't fathom why the police were making themselves visible to me. It was like he was trying to bully me into a confession.

"Why are you still being interrogated?"

I didn't answer immediately, so she grabbed my hand and said, "Talk to me. You keep giving me bits and pieces. What the hell is really going on?"

I gave her the short version. It was way more detailed causing Brina to be shaken.

"You might be going to jail and you're going about life like nothing happened?"

"Trust me, not a day goes by that I don't think about this shit. I had no choice. They were going to kill us," I said whispering. "Look, we can talk about this later."

"Okay," she said, like she was disappointed in me.

Brina and I watched as Detective Berry turned his car around at the end of my parking lot, backed into a space and just sat there with the engine running.

Seconds later, the Infiniti came rolling around the corner. It was Yaya's dumb ass again. She drove down near Detective Berry's car and rolled down her window. I didn't even look over in their direction to see if they were talking to one another, but it appeared to me they knew one another. I tried my best to act like their presence wasn't even bothering me. Inside though, I was a wreck. They were bold as fuck to be in front of my apartment building. What the hell did they have in common?

Yaya was determined, however, to make sure everyone saw her. She walked over to us looking like a Madam demanding I give her some money. As I was trying to figure out what this bitch was on, Detective Berry drove out of the parking lot smiling as if he knew what was going on.

"It's payday, bitches," she shouted.

"Zsa, who is this whore?" Brina asked.

Before I could answer, Yaya completely went all New York on us.

"Bitch, I'm Yaya from Farragut Projects. Wife to one…O.B. You better recognize. Brooklyn all day, Boo," Yaya said, swinging her long braids from side to side.

"Look, all that New York lingo is a complete waste of time on me and my friend here. We grew up in Virginia Beach. We use words like dude," I said.

"Oh and don't forget, Boy. We call everyone 'boy'. Sorta like how y'all use the word son," Brina joked.

Brina and I looked at each other and fell out laughing.

Was this bitch serious? We didn't give a fuck where she was from or who she was married to, for real.

Yaya was absolutely comical to me; from the different shades of hair color, to the long ghetto nail art, to how she talked. She needed her own reality show if you asked me.

What was even more comical was how scared of her O.B was. A real nigga would've had this bitch shut down a long time ago regardless of what she had on them. But I guess if he wanted to see his son again he had to play by her rules for now.

With a big vein running down the middle of his forehead, I could see O.B coming from afar. He gritted his teeth, and walked over at a swift pace.

"Oh, so you just happen to be drivin' by, huh?" she asked him.

"Why you out here buggin'?"

"Why you still hangin' around this bitch?"

"Look, you need to leave."

When he attempted to grab her by the arm, she looked down and said, "So you tryin' to put hands on me now...ok...you must think this a damn game?" She pulled out her phone and dialed a number.

"Yeah...hold on...someone wants to talk to you."

She handed O.B the phone. He stared at her for a moment.

"Yeah...who dis?" he said.

"It's me, Daddy," O.B's son replied.

With tears forming in the corner of his eyes, O.B had a look of defeat on his face.

"Daddy?"

"What up little man? How you been?"

Before his son could answer, Yaya snatched the phone out of his hands and hung up. I thought O.B was going to kill her right in front of us. He lunged, jumped on her, grabbed her by the neck and started choking her. What was making him angry was the fact that she laughed the whole time. This woman was truly evil and it was only a matter of time before it was going to be game over for her.

After pleading with O.B to let Yaya go, Brina and I tried to drag him in my apartment. Before he would go in, he dug in his pockets, pulled out a wad of cash and threw it at her.

"Here crab bitch, your payment!"

I had no idea exactly how much he'd thrown at her, but my eyes registered at least twenty hundred dollar bills. I couldn't wait to find out what she really had over him.

"I got your bitch," she yelled, as she scooped the bills up off the ground. "I hope you enjoyed talkin' to yo' son cause that's the last time you will ever hear from him again mothafucka…because you… aaaand that bitch will be in jail soon," she said, laughing as she walked away.

As soon as we got O.B in the house, I grabbed my phone and called the one person who I knew could shut Yaya down. I hated to do it, but it was the only thing I could think of. While the phone rang, I thought of my upbringing. I knew what I was doing wasn't right, but the knock at the door confirmed my actions.

His voice mail came on, "Call me," I said then ended the call. "It's important."

The knock at the door didn't even startle me because I was ready for round two with Yaya. The nerve of that bitch to knock on my door. I grabbed the door knob, ready to fight.

"What the fuck do you want, bitch? You don't want to fuck with me, Yaya," I screamed, as I swung the door back. To my surprise, Yaya was long gone. There stood a tall, lean and pale woman with file folders and a raggedy pocketbook.

Shit, I was not ready for this. I'd only been here a few days, I thought. I quickly took the scarf off of my head and welcomed her in as best I could, considering the circumstances. Brina and O.B scattered away as soon as they saw the size of my eyes, huge was an understatement.

"Hello, Mrs. Jones. I am Mrs. Davis, your appointed social worker. I look forward to working with you and helping you get your son back," she said, as she walked in and glanced around, stepping to the side so I could take the lead. She looked uncomfortable and rightfully so, this lady was witnessing organized crime, for Christ sakes.

After leading her to the living room, we took a seat on the couch to talk. She explained why she was there, which I already knew, and asked for a tour of my apartment.

"This is the room Ryan will be sleeping in," I said, walking into Ryan and Zeta's room. At one point, while living with my mother, we all slept in the same room. This was definitely a come up and Ryan would be so excited to see how I decorated his side of the room. I could sense her discomfort; catching her look over her shoulder more than once.

I showed her the den that was filled with toys. When we went back down to the living room, she told me how nice the place looked. I was so relieved and my hopes were high. But then my hopes faded when she told me that even after she made her recommendations, there was still no guarantee I would get Ryan back. I guess the sad look on my face made her feel sorry for me.

"Mrs. Jones, you need to keep the faith. Stay out of trouble. Keep your job and you should be good."

"Okay, thank you," I said, even though I felt the rug had been pulled from under my feet.

We were just finishing up our visit, when O.B walked in ranting about how tired he was of Yaya blackmailing him. I excused myself quickly and ran to the den to tell him to shut the hell up. As I was coming back, I saw the social worker writing something down in her notes with a worried look on her face. Brina was peeking around the corner, being more supportive than anything.

"Well, Mrs. Jones, I'll be in touch," the social worker said in a low voice, as she got up looking toward the den. I followed her to the door like a lost puppy.

As soon as I closed the door behind her, I walked into the den and smacked the shit out of O.B. I was glad Cindy was not there because she would have tried to intervene but at this point, I no longer cared. I was sorry Brina had to witness my rage but his ass was grass to me.

"What the hell you do that for?" he roared, holding his face.

"Because you probably just fucked up my chance of getting my son back," I yelled, before I stormed up the steps to my room. "And, why the hell are you walking up in here like you own the place? Last time I checked, this was me and Cindy's apartment. Get your own shit, freeloader," I said, not giving a fuck.

Brina marched right along with me, staring O.B down like a mad woman.

nineteen...

The next day at work, Vicki asked me what time I was going to be ready for our fun weekend that I'd evidently forgotten all about.

"Ready for what," I asked.

"You're supposed to go out tonight."

Upset, I shook my head. I forgot she wanted me to meet her boyfriend ,Tee's, brother. Honestly, I had so much shit going on in my life I didn't even give it a second thought after she asked me. I had spoken to Tee a couple of times at the store and he seemed cool. I'm sure his brother probably was too but I just wasn't feeling it. Thinking about the home visit with the social worker and the detective watching me, I couldn't keep my mind from racing. *If only the pills worked for my depression and anxiety, I would be okay,* I thought.

"I don't know if I can make it, I don't have a babysitter."

"Ask Cindy," she said.

I didn't want to ask Cindy because she was always laid up with O.B, but Vicki insisted because she'd already told him I would go out with him.

"Well, just tell him I can't."

"Fine," she said, grabbing the phone.

I thought about it for a moment. "Wait. Let me see what I can do when I get home."

I needed to be revived and a date with a handsome guy

might just do the trick so I rushed to Brenda's, picked up Zeta and headed home.

After putting my purse down, I heard laughter coming from the den, so I made my way there. As usual, Cindy and O.B were snuggled up on the couch.

"Do you two have any plans tonight?" I asked, plopping down in the chair.

"No, we're just gonna watch a movie. Why?" Cindy said.

I asked her to baby-sit and she was more than happy to.

I was so nervous, I completely demolished my closet. I was going on my first real date. I didn't know what to wear because I wasn't sure where we were going. So, I played it safe and decided on my chocolate, Michael Kors halter dress and matching sling back sandals.

I stood in front of the mirror admiring how nice the dress made my ass look. Then I went downstairs. As I was changing purses, I could hear Cindy on the phone. She was talking in riddles and the call seemed to have her on edge. I made a mental note to ask her later why she was so frazzled. She quickly got off the phone when she realized I was within hearing distance. Cindy complimented me on how pretty I looked, but pretty wasn't the look I was going for. She turned to O.B to ask him how I looked. It was written all over his face. I could feel his eyes burning holes right through my dress.

"She looks aight," he answered with tight lips.

Poor Cindy was so naive. She figured he was jealous because of the thought of another man touching his sister, not realizing he was upset about another man being with his ex-girlfriend.

My phone alerted me that I had a text. I was hoping he wanted to cancel on me. I almost forgot that Londa gave this dude my number. However, the text read: **I'm outside**. I began to get nervous like I was a teenager going out on my first date.

"I'll see you guys later," I said, as I pranced to the door. I kissed Zeta on the way out and checked my makeup one last time before leaving. His big boy Benz was several cars away so

I peered over at it in an attempt to get a glimpse of my date. As I neared the car, a guy emerged to greet me wearing Hugo Boss fitted pants, a Polo shirt, and loafers. The weather was balmy and a perfect night for a first date.

I took about two more steps and stopped dead in my tracks, but my date was already moving towards me. I spun around on my heels, ready to go back in the house with heat coming from my ears. Out of all the men in Richmond, she set me up with this fool.

"So, Jazzy, we meet again," he said with a smile.

This couldn't be happening. I was so shocked to see Dolo standing there in front of me. I just stood there for a minute in complete silence. To his credit, he did look like he had just stepped out of a GQ magazine.

"So, you're my date," I asked.

"I guess so. Is that a problem?" I hesitated so he continued. "If it makes you feel any better, I'm just as surprised as you," he said.

For some reason, I didn't think so. I felt like he set this whole thing up. I was already dressed and it was just dinner so I got in the car and prayed the night went by quickly.

During dinner, I was surprised that Dolo wasn't the asshole he portrayed himself to be. He actually made me laugh a couple of times but you could tell that he could be a very intense person if he had to be. He told me all about his life growing up in New York and how he was very poor growing up and all about he and his brother's fiascos. My guess was that's why he was dealing drugs. Once you've been that poor, you do what you have to, to not be in that situation again.

We finished dinner, had dessert and an after dinner drink, then we left the restaurant. I only lived ten minutes from the restaurant so the drive home was quick. I stepped out of the car and walked around to the driver's side door. Dolo pushed open the door and stood in front of me.

"Thank you for dinner. I had a good time."

He tilted his head to the side. "Why are you so uneasy

around me?"

"Well, I guess it started when you came in the store and got nasty with me. And then I saw you at the club and I don't know if you know it or not, but you almost shot me."

"I almost shot you? How did I almost shoot you?" he asked in amazement.

Really? Oh, so now you have selective memory? I thought.

"Well, I just happened to be standing right next to you when you shot at those guys that night at Aqua."

"First of all, those niggas started shooting at me."

"Well, when you started shooting back, I was standing right next to you."

"No wonder you were acting so strange at dinner. Well, since you gave me a fake name and number at the club, can't we just call it even?" He flashed a wide grin and we both laughed.

We stared at each other for a few seconds and then he broke the awkwardness by saying, "Hopefully, you'll forgive me and go out with me again."

"We'll see," I said with a smirk. *What was I saying?* I thought. I turned away. "I'm tired and I have to work tomorrow, so I better go."

As I walked to my door, I took one last look at him. I forgot all about the bad boy lifestyle. Instead, my thoughts went straight to his physical looks. He looked so good with his broad shoulders and muscular arms. "Zsaset, snap out of it girl," I whispered.

I was so glad that Zeta was sleeping when I walked into the house. Cindy and O.B were still up but they were in her room so I was thankful I didn't have to answer any questions about my date. I wasn't exactly looking forward to seeing the reactions on their faces when I told them I went out with Dolo. I went up to my bathroom, washed off my makeup, slid into my Victoria's Secret Pink pajamas and tried to get some sleep.

I guess sleep wasn't in the cards for me because I was up half the night thinking about my evening with

Dolo. I enjoyed talking to him, even though I shouldn't have been in his company. Scary as it was, I knew I would see him again whether I wanted to or not.

Vicki had gotten me into this situation so I called to curse her ass out for hooking me up with Dolo.

"Hi, Zsaset. How was your night? I hope it was as good as mine," she said, sounding spaced out.

"Somehow? I doubt it," I said angrily.

"Did you forget who I was with tonight?"

"C'mon, Zsaset, everything went okay. You got home safe, didn't you?"

"Yes, I did. That's not the point. You set me up with a drug dealer, slash killer. I mean, weren't you the one who told me how crazy he was?"

"I'm sorry, but he paid me a lot of money to hook y'all up. He really likes you."

"Bitch, you pimped me out?" I asked. I knew from the jump that was a set-up.

"Please don't be mad but I had bills to pay and he kept going on and on about how gorgeous you were. Come on, so you're telling me, his bad boy image didn't turn you on, at all?"

"Not even a little bit." Still frustrated, I went on, "Why do I even talk to you?"

"Uh-huh. I knew it. You wanted him, didn't you?"

"Vicki, I'm gonna act like I didn't hear you say that."

"Okay. I'll let that be our little secret," she said in a playful tone.

"Bye, bitch. I have to get up early so I can go see Ryan."

"Okay, let me know how it goes."

Normally Dolo would not be my pick of the litter, but when you're batting zero, the bottom of the barrel looks good.

I Shoulda' SEEN HIM Coming

• • •

At 7:00 a.m., I stumbled out of the bed in my wife beater and boy shorts. I wanted to get to Norfolk and back home before the evening traffic. I quickly showered and dressed. Then it was Zeta's turn. *I forgot to tell Zeta we were scheduled to see Ryan today,* I thought suddenly.

"Mommy, where we going? I'm still sleepy."

"I know baby, but don't you want to see your brother?"

"I'm going to see Ryan?"

"You sure are."

Once she knew she was going to see her brother, she lit up. She even started rushing me. I hadn't been home in months and couldn't wait to see Ryan, my mom and my home girls. Deonte hadn't called and I was tactually thankful for that. It was strange, though.

By 9:00 a.m., we were on the road headed to Norfolk. I was happy and nervous at the same time. I guess it was because I didn't know what to expect. I arrived at the address Mrs. Smith gave me and was surprised that the foster family's house was in an exclusive neighborhood. I'm going to have a hard time getting Ryan to leave this place. Better yet, I want to be put in foster care. I walked up the sidewalk and rang the doorbell. When the woman opened the door, Ryan was standing next to her, holding onto her pants.

"Hey boo," I said, giving him a big hug.

He shyly spoke back, then he grabbed Zeta and gave her a big hug and a kiss. They immediately started playing around.

We stayed for about an hour, and the whole time Ryan probably said three words to me. I didn't understand why he was acting so weird. My first thought was maybe he was mad at me for leaving him with my mom. Then I thought he was probably mad because he felt we both deserted him. Before I left, I reassured him I would be back for him because I had my own

158

place and he and Zeta had their own room. I told him how it was decorated with his favorite toys and I had Transformer sheets on the bed for him. He smiled briefly, gave me a kiss, and then walked off.

I was at the front door digging around in my oversized bag for my keys, when Mrs. Smith came in. I guess she had another child placed at the home in addition to Ryan. She was the last person I wanted to talk to.

"Hello, Mrs. Jones," she said like she was tired of seeing me.

"Hi, Mrs. Smith," I said, trying to be respectful.

I told her how my visit went but she wasn't concerned about that, at all. The first thing she did was remind me of the previous warning that if there were anymore mishaps, she would take him from me, for good. Surprisingly, after her lecture, she told me what I needed to do to get him back. She said she understood that I was just having a little bad luck.

"I can tell how much you love your children. That's the only reason I'm cutting you a break. But this is it. So, get your shit together." I was shocked when she cursed at me like we were friends but I guess I needed it. "I'll be making my decision next week on when you can get him back. You're going to have an unscheduled visit, so be ready."

"I will. Thank you so much." Mrs. Smith was one person who put fear in my heart. Afterwards, when I went by my mom's apartment, I told her how cold Ryan was towards me. She reminded me that Ryan had been through a lot through the years, especially with me and Deonte.

She said, "As soon as he gets up there with you and Zeta, he'll be fine."

Leave it to my mom to make me feel better even though her Lupus was making her so sick she couldn't even walk. I wanted to help her as much as I could so I made a few casseroles for her and froze them. I also picked up a few of her favorite pastries from the local bakery. I smiled, knowing the simplest things still brought comfort to her. Then I washed a couple of loads of clothes, dried them, folded them and put them away.

"Well, Ma...I need to get on the road before I get caught in traffic."

"Okay, baby. I'm so glad you and Zeta came by to see me. Call me more often, hear? I want you to take care of yourself and do right so you can get our boy back."

I gave her a kiss and I told her I would. I left my mom's house then stopped by to pick up my girl Sheba before I hit the road. Then my phone started to vibrate. I reached inside my purse to find it. It was a text from Nicole. I had Siri read me the message.

"Hey Z, when you get in town, stop by my house. I need to talk to you about something," Siri said loudly.

"What the hell is that all about?" Sheba yelled. "That shit don't make sense at all. That bitch won't even answer our calls."

I personally hadn't spoken to Nicole since I left Norfolk and now she had something to tell me. I didn't understand why she just didn't call me. It was weird even for Nicole; someone I've learned to expect just about anything from.

I persuaded Sheba to ride with me over to Nicole's but first we needed to make a quick stop at McDonald's to get something to eat. So I texted Nicole back and let her know I would be there in twenty minutes.

Siri replied, **"Ok."**

I placed my order first. "May I have a large fry and a large coffee with fifteen sugars and three creams?"

Sheba laughed loudly. "You and your damn fifteen sugars. Why fifteen, Z? Why not fourteen or sixteen?" We both chuckled. "I mean, who the hell does that? How the hell did you determine you needed fifteen, you counted them bitches one day and remembered them for future reference?"

I couldn't help but laugh and shake my head. "Shut the hell up, crazy ass. Worry 'bout your burger with three extra pickles."

Laughing about us both having our own little preferences

and having a good time with one another, we headed over to Nicole's.

When we arrived at Nicole's house, Sheba told me she wasn't getting out so I could just leave Zeta in the car with her.

"Don't act like that. Come in and at least say hello," I said, trying to play peace maker.

"Tell her hi for me and no thank you to your invite to go in that crazy girl's house. I will stay with Miss Zeta," she said, turning the music up louder. Zeta was bobbing her head to the beat. That little girl was growing up way too fast for me.

"Fine."

When I got out of my car, I noticed Ms. Ida, my mother's friend, sweeping the porch across from Nicole's house. I walked over to her and spoke. She gave me the biggest hug and told me how glad she was to see me.

"I thought you lived in Norview," I commented.

'I did but it was gettin' too bad over there so my children bought me this house over a year ago.

"Oh, I had no idea."

"It's smaller and one floor. That's what I needed on account of my leg and hip."

We talked for a bit then I realized that my mom said she saw Deonte across from Ms. Ida's house.

"Do you remember which house my mom saw Deonte at?" I asked.

"Well, he wasn't at a house when we seen him. He was just parked on the side over there in front of that blue house," she said, pointing to the house next to Nicole's.

Neither my mom nor Ms. Ida were good witnesses. They were both over seventy and both wore bifocals. I felt there was no need to keep questioning her since I'd gotten away from him, and didn't plan on rekindling shit. Besides, Nicole would've called me a long time ago if she'd seen Deonte in her neighborhood.

After saying my goodbyes to Ms. Ida, I walked up to Nicole's door but before I could knock, I noticed the door was ajar so I just walked in.

"Nicole, it's me, Zsa!" I yelled.

No response.

"Nicole!"

No response again.

As I headed upstairs, I could hear voices, but I couldn't make out what was being said. When I reached the top stairs, I could see that Nicole's bedroom door was slightly opened, so I entered the room. I could not believe my own eyes.

My first thought was to throw something.

Then I wondered where was the nearest knife.

Nicole was bent over on the bed as Deonte was penetrating her backside. Unaware of my presence, Deonte continued to dig deeper into Nicole as he spread her ass cheeks.

Nicole glanced over and before she could say a word, I was storming towards the bed. *I'd always known Nicole was a hoe, but Deonte? Why?*

All kinds of crazy thoughts filled my head. No wonder he hadn't been bugging me; his dirty ass was busy fucking Nicole. I said a silent prayer that he rot in hell before busting them both in the head.

"Y'all cruddy mothafuckers!" I screamed as I hit Deonte in the side of the face with a lamp.

Deonte jumped and backed away from me as Nicole grabbed a sheet off the bed and began to make her plea.

"Z, I'm sorry. Wait...wait, let us explain," Nicole said, trying to cover up.

"Bitch, the fuck you mean, wait?"

"Zsaset, what are you doing here? How did you get in?" Deonte asked.

"Mothafucka, don't worry about that. What the fuck are you doing fuckin' my damn friend?" I said, swinging at him again. He grabbed my arm and held it in the air.

"I can't believe y'all. This is how you do me! Get the fuck off me, Deonte!"

I kneed Deonte in his balls and lunged at Nicole. We

began to tussle. Losing her balance, Nicole tripped over the sheet and fell on the floor. That's when I started pulling her by the hair. We both were throwing fists and yelling. It was total chaos.

Minutes later, Deonte finally regained feeling between his legs and was able to pull us apart.

"Look, chill out, both of you," he demanded.

"Just leave, Zsaset," Nicole begged.

"Bitch, I would've never even come over this bitch if you hadn't texted me and told me to."

Deonte's shoulders slumped. "You told her to come over here?"

He looked like he wanted to kill Nicole.

"Yes, she did," I yelled as I charged her again. This bitch was too foul for my taste and that was saying a lot.

Nicole looked proud, like she had solved a mystery but this bitch was dead to me. Taking her down wasn't an option, it was a necessity.

"Give it up, Z! Why you actin' so mad? It's not like you wanted his ass anyway. Get over it!"

"You were my friend, bitch! Real friends don't fuck each other's men unless you're a thot."

"I guess we were never friends then," she said with a devilish grin."

I picked up the glass vase on the table and threw it at her and said, "I guess that's why your whoring ass needs this then!"

The glass shattered everywhere; water and flowers painted the room. Instantly, I picked up a piece of glass from the floor, and slashed her face before she could get away.

As blood gushed, I told her, "Now every time you fuck Deonte, he'll see your face and think of me."

As Nicole held her face, screaming like crazy, I glared at Deonte, "You can forget ever seeing your daughter again, mothafucka!"

I gave Nicole one more smack to the face and then walked out. That bitch set herself up sending me a text. She thought the joke was on me; instead she's got a mark for life.

I could hear the two of them arguing as I rushed out. Nicole wanted to call the cops on me, but Deonte said, nah, not my Zeta's mother. I laughed at the irony as I jetted to the car. Deonte went too far this time and I was going to make his ass suffer for it. Answering his apology calls, if they even came, was not going to happen and seeing Zeta was out of the question.

It all made sense. This asshole was busy fucking a friend of mine senseless, showing his true colors. At one point, I really thought Deonte loved me and would eventually grow up and be a good father to Zeta. His ass was crazy if he thought I was going to fuck with him in the slightest way, even if he sought custody of Zeta.

At that very moment a text came through.Of course, he didn't have the balls to call, but he could text me a sob story, in all caps, too.

ZSASET, I'M SORRY. I HOPE YOU WILL FORGIVE ME FOR THE SAKE OF OUR CHILD. HOPE YOU WILL LET ME SEE ZETA.

Blah, Blah, Blah, I thought. He took 'fucked up' to a whole new level and would never see Zeta again if it was up to me. I would deal with Deonte later. It was 'me' time and I was putting my plan in action. Getting ahead was all I desired.

twenty...

A couple of days went by with me sulking about what had been going on in my life. It was raining hard so Cindy and I decided to stay home since she knew how I was feeling. It was the first time the apartment had been that quiet since we moved in. I played a few games with Zeta until she fell asleep. Feeling depressed and still turnt up from my altercation with Nicole, I took off my clothes, slipped into some leggings and a t-shirt, tied a scarf around my head and went downstairs. I needed to tell my mom and Brina about that tramp Nicole. I knew my mom wasn't feeling well so I decided I would tell her later, but Brina needed to know now. After all, we were all like sisters. As soon as she answered the phone, I went in. She couldn't believe it.

"I'm in shock right now," Brina said.

"How you think I feel seeing my husband and one of my so-called best friends fucking?" I said on the brink of crying. "Brina, be honest with me…did you know?"

"Let me tell your ass something. If I had known, I would've beat that bitch's ass then came and told you so you could whip her ass. I don't play that shit."

"Exactly and that's why I fucked her ass up."

"Good, that bitch knows we don't ever let dick come between us. We're like family."

I felt a little bit guilty about the feelings I was having for

K-Dog and I didn't want to be a hypocrite so I asked her about her feelings for him.

"Girl, some people are just meant to be friends. We're just not meshing as a couple but I'm cool with that. Especially since I just met this guy from Atlanta."

"Whaaattt?" I asked.

"Yes, honey. I think he just might be the one."

"Awwww…I'm so happy for you."

"Thanks."

We talked a little more, then hung up. Prepared for an evening of television and popcorn, I curled up on the couch. With a Heineken in one hand and remote in the other, I flipped the channels only to find nothing on. I was so bored, I found myself hypnotized by the hard falling rain that hit the roof. It was getting dark so I got off the couch to close the blinds. As I was closing the blinds, I saw a man dressed in all black watching me a few feet from my window. *Oh my, God! Who the fuck is that?* I couldn't see his face, but he was wearing black sweat pants with red stripes running down the sides.

Shaking, I quickly closed the blinds and pulled my drapes together then I ran to the kitchen and grabbed a knife. I ran upstairs and looked out the window to get a better look but the guy was gone. *What if he tries to kick my door in?* I thought, so I started back down the stairs to prop a chair up under the door knob. When I reached the last step there was a knock at the door. I stared at the doorknob for a few seconds before I moved. I stood up against the wall as my knees buckled.

"Who is it?" I yelled.

There was no response so I put my eye against the peep-hole. My view was obstructed by someone's finger. I slowly crept to the window but I didn't see anyone.

"Who is it?" I asked again, getting pissed. Still, there was no answer. "All right, let's see if you say something when I put one in your ass," I said calling the person's bluff.

"Girl, it's me, Dolo."

Oh my, God. What is he doing here? "Umm. One

minute," I said as I pulled the scarf off of my head.

I opened the door and there he was, standing in front of me wearing a gray tracksuit and Jordans. "Hi, what brings you by?"

"I was in the neighborhood and decided to drop in. I hope that's okay," he said with a smile that made me want to melt.

"I guess. Come on in."

Dolo was drenched from the rain. I took his umbrella and sat it behind the door. As I closed the door, I looked around for the mystery person and could have sworn I saw someone disappear in to the woods. The thought of someone I didn't know being that close to me unnerved me.

"I haven't talked to you in a while. Where have you been?" I asked, trying to act normal and not bring attention to my fucked up life.

"I had to make a run up top. As a matter of fact, I just got back about an hour ago," he said, sitting on the couch like he owned the place. This nigga is definitely a boss, I thought, taking notice of his gold and diamond encrusted necklace!

"Hey, did you see the guy that was just in front of my window?" I asked.

"No…there's no one out there. Well, there wasn't when I came up anyway."

"Maybe I'm imagining things but I could've sworn I saw this guy who's been following me."

"Why is he following you?"

"I don't know. I'm not even sure he's following me. I saw him in the food court watching me about three weeks ago. It could just be a coincidence that I keep running into him." I wanted to call the cops but the cops were after me. This situation was fucked up and I felt like the walls were caving in on me.

I offered Dolo something to drink for what turned out to be a really long night. We talked for hours about our personal lives. I guess he was starting to feel comfortable around me because he dropped the bomb that he and Tee had been abandoned by their junkie mother when they were three and five years old and grew up in an orphanage. I didn't know why but people always wanted to tell me their darkest secrets.

By the time we finished our conversation, I understood why he was fucked up in the head. We really didn't have too much in common. I guess that's what drew us together. They say opposites attract.

It was three o' clock in the morning when the credits rolled to the movie we were watching. We both fought back sleep. I eased a few inches away from Dolo. "Well, I'm about to turn in," I said yawning.

"Yeah, I better get going. It's raining kind of hard and I live across town."

I guess he was trying to drop me a hint so I decided to be nice. I would've felt bad if he had gotten hurt in an accident so I asked him if he wanted to stay for the night. It was only a couple of hours before morning anyway."

"You sure?" he asked.

"Yeah. C'mon, we can go up to my room. I'll make you a bed on the floor."

When we got upstairs to my room, he pulled his hoodie over his head and threw it on my chaise.

Standing near my bed, he stopped and squinted.

"What's wrong?" I asked, alarmed.

"What's that stickin' out from your bed?"

I looked down at my bed to see what he was talking about.

"Oh, that's a knife. I keep it for protection."

"What the hell a knife gonna do? You need a gun."

"Absolutely not! My daughter might get to it."

"You can keep it locked up."

Maybe having a gun wasn't such a bad idea. It was something to definitely think about. I just didn't want to think about it at that moment. I was way too mentally exhausted.

I layered the floor with blankets and quilts. He was so

tired he slipped under the blankets like he was sleeping on a Serta. By the time I returned from the bathroom, he was knocked out cold and snoring like a fat man. For just a moment, Dolo had a sort of an angelic innocence about him. Instead of a bad boy, he actually resembled a baby boy.

Dolo and Zeta were already up by the time I awoke. "Good morning, Mommy," Zeta said.

"Good morning, baby. Whatcha watchin'?"

"I'm watchin' cartoons wit the man," she said.

"I see," I said, staring at Dolo.

"Well, I hate to break up your little party but I have to get to work. And Miss Zeta Beta you have to go to Brenda's."

"I don't wanna go, Mommy."

"I know, but Mommy has to go make some money."

Feeling sorry for Zeta, Dolo said, "Why don't you just take the day off?"

"Everybody can't live like you ...Mr. Don Corleone." I could tell his ego was pumped by the way he smiled. It really tripped me out how Italian mafia criminals were always super heroes to the boys in the hood.

He reached in his pants pocket and pulled out a handful of money. He then proceeded to peel off ten, one hundred dollar bills and handed them to me.

"What is this for?" I asked.

"You said you wished you could take the day off, but you have to pay bills, right? Now you can take the day off and still pay your bills."

I wasn't sure if I should keep the money, but I was tired and a day off from work was what I needed. I thanked him and walked him downstairs to the door.

"Can I see you later?" he asked.

"I don't see why not. But can you keep this between me and you?" I asked. Dolo's smirk was filled with many questions. "I have my reasons and one of them is that I don't like people all up in my business."

"I see. Well, will you explain your other reasons to me?"

"Maybe later."

He kissed me on the lips and left. "Thanks," he said, as he walked away.

"Thanks for what," I inquired. He stopped and turned around.

"For not judgin' me like everyone else. I'm really not all that bad."

"Yeah, well that still remains to be seen." I smiled seductively and closed the door.

After calling out, I spent the whole day with Zeta. I also needed some time to myself so I dropped her off at Brenda's for the night. On the way back home, I stopped at the convenience store in the strip mall of our complex to get a beer and some snacks. I threw my car in park and jumped out. I was walking in the store when I felt a sudden chill that ran up my spine. When I looked slightly to my right, I noticed the guy with the scar staring at me.

His stare was so unsettling and emotionless, I immediately knew I had seen him before. It was the guy from the food court. I looked him up and down and noticed he had on black pants with a red stripe. *Oh shit! That's who was peeking in my window.* I held my purse tightly against my body and walked into the store as I dialed K-Dog's number. It went to voicemail. "Dog, it's Zsa. Something weird is going on. Call me when you get this message." I stuck my hand in my purse and pulled out my knife. I didn't want to hurt anyone else but I would if I had to.

I was so busy on the phone, I didn't notice that he had followed me into the store. I quickly grabbed my sandwiches and drinks and headed to the checkout counter. As I stood there waiting to be rung up, his eyes were stuck on me for a few seconds then he left the store. He was really starting to freak me out because I didn't know what his intentions were.

As I was walking to my car, I noticed a piece of paper on my windshield. My first thought was it was probably somebody selling something. I pulled my wiper blade back and quickly grabbed the note. I thought I was going to have a panic attack right then and there when the note read 'I know what you did Bitch and you're gonna pay for it.' I immediately looked around but no one but the creepy guy was standing outside. Confronting him was out of the question so I jumped in my car and locked the doors.

He watched me leave the parking space with this bizarre look in his eyes. Something was definitely not right with this dude and I had a sick feeling that it had something to do with me and something I had done. I wanted so badly to say something smart to him but I was truly scared of him. He knew it, too.

I returned home to find Cindy and O.B all over each other on the living room floor.

"Y'all need to take that shit up to your room," I said.

Cindy laughed and said, "That's where we're about to go."

O.B ran up the steps but Cindy stayed in the living room with me for a few minutes to catch up on the Ryan situation.

"So, have they said anything yet?"

"Not yet, Mrs. Smith should be calling any day now."

About ten minutes into our conversation, there was a knock at the door. I could hear Cindy telling the visitor I was in the living room. I peeked around the corner and it was Dolo.

"Hey, I thought you were gonna be tied down ...I mean tied up all night," I said jokingly. He laughed.

"Oh you got jokes, huh? I'm actually free for the rest of the night so I decided to stop by. I hope that's okay."

Didn't he say the same shit last night? I hope he doesn't make it a habit of just popping up whenever he feels like it, I thought.

"Sure, sit down. We're just having a little girl time. By the way, this is my brother's girlfriend Cindy."

He spoke and then sat next to me on the love seat. I could tell Cindy was uncomfortable so I asked her to help me get some beers from the fridge.

"Girl, you didn't tell me you're messin' with Dolo," Cindy said shocked.

I wanted to tell the bitch to mind her business but I kept cool about it. "I didn't tell anyone because I'm not messing with him, we're just chillin'."

"Uh-hum. I bet," she said, twisting her lips.

She was about to say something else when a text came through. As she was reading it, I could sense that it made her a little on edge. She waited for a few minutes before she responded as if she had to carefully think about what she wanted to say. I made another mental note about Cindy's strange ways.

"Is everything okay?" I asked.

"Oh yeah. It's just work."

"You're not a very good liar. You know that?"

"I promise you, everything is okay. Now back to you and Dolo. Zsaset, did you see the ice on his watch?"

"Yeah, I did. It's not about the money. It's about the man behind the money," I said laughing.

"Oh, okay. I gotchu. He's fine as hell, though."

"I know. That's what's keeping my interest," I teased.

"You be careful, girl. He's a big time hustler." She got serious.

"Oh, don't worry. A sista can take care of herself."

After our conversation, Cindy seemed more relaxed.

I wanted a little more privacy so I invited Dolo up to my room. This time I had no plans to make him a bed on the floor. He was going to sleep with me that night. It had been a long time since a man held me. And no matter how much I tried to deny it, I wanted that feeling again.

I knew that our relationship could never amount to much, but I was going to enjoy it for as long as it lasted.

"So, what side do you want?" I asked.

"The side you're on," he said in a sexy tone.

I winked and sashayed towards the bathroom. "Get comfortable. I'll be back shortly," I said.

I twisted the knob in the shower. The water steamed just

the way I liked it. Tonight would be special. So, I lathered my body with a mixture of Jasmine Vanilla and Cotton Blossom body wash, compliments of Bath & Body Works. I gave my legs a close shave for a smooth touch. When I got out of the shower, I slipped on my Victoria's Secret sexy black one piece. I appeared from behind the door and Dolo's yo-yo expression was priceless. He laid on the bed speechless and dumbfounded.

"What's wrong," I asked, pretending not to know.

He didn't reply at first because he was too busy drooling at my breasts. After letting out a heavy sigh, he replied, "Nothing."

"I take it you like what you see."

"Hell, yeah. I like it a lot."

He tried hard not to stare, but it was too impossible. The sight was enough to make a blind man see. The lady at the store told me I would get this type of reaction and she was right. I slid in the bed and pulled just enough covers over me to tease him.

Afraid to make the first move, I waited for him. Ten minutes passed, and I was still waiting. Don't tell me this nigga is gay. Dolo just laid there under the sheets.

"You know, when I told you not to try anything," I said breaking the silence, "Well ... umm ...I was just playing."

"I know. I just don't want you to think that this is all I want from you," he said.

"I can get some ass from any girl I want. Unfortunately, I can't get friends as easily. That's what I want with you. I haven't been this comfortable with someone in a long time. Believe it or not, I value our friendship."

"Okay, I'm all for being friends and shit but right now I need some dick. We can be friends afterwards."

"Whatever you say," he laughed.

I wasn't prepared for what was about to happen. Dolo caught me totally off guard. He crawled like a P.O.W. to the edge of the bed. *What is he doing?* I thought. When my ass was at the bottom of my mattress, then I knew. Dolo had yanked me by the ankles. With one hard pull, my one piece flew off like it was attached with Velcro. I thought he was losing his mind. This nightie cost too much money for him to be destroying it. He was so rough it scared me.

I attempted to kiss Dolo, but he pushed back my forehead with his hands. What he did next went overboard. He stroked his fingers in and out of my mouth as if he was finger-fucking my face. I didn't know where the hell his fingers been. I was so turned off.

"Baby, slow down," I gagged as he slowly pulled them out one at a time.

"Look, this is my show. You gotta play by my rules," he groaned.

I decided to be a pawn in his game. Didn't he know sex was a two way street? Dolo flipped me on my stomach and instantly began licking the soles of my feet. That made me wet as hell. His hands slid up my inner thigh. They felt like a hundred fingers gripping my flesh from all angles. When air hit the middle of my cheeks, I held on for dear life. He swirled his tongue around the inner wall of my ass. At the same time, he rammed his fingers inside my booty. One finger, two fingers, three ...I screamed at the top of my lungs. Clawing at the headboard, I tried to get away, but he snatched me back down.

Slamming me onto my back and gripping my titties roughly, he wasted no time plunging his dick in me. The friction from his thickness scraped my sugarwalls and my booty felt like it was on fire. I wrapped my legs around his back, trying to get into his rhythm, moving fast; up and down, again and again. Dolo pulled out, forcefully grabbed my shoulders and pushed me down to my knees. Sick as it may sound; his forcefulness was such a turn on.

He pushed my head forward and the hard edge of the bedpost caught me under the chin. I sucked enthusiastically on his jimmy like a hungry baby on a bottle of Kool-Aid. Damn, I felt like porno ho. Fire burned between my legs. He pressed my head deeper and deeper until he was all in. Massaging his balls, I made him soar into another level. He shouted like a girl. I did it. I finally had him at my mercy. I had a sense of satisfaction. I felt like this man was going to be my destruction and those feelings proved to be right.

twenty-one...

Two weeks later July 10th rolled around; my birthday. As a gift to myself, I bought a 2013 Mercedes CLK 320 Convertible. Well, K-Dog and Quan looked out and gifted it to me. Hell, they had to do something with the drug money they were getting. The first place I hit was Vicki's house. She wasn't home. *Where the hell is everyone? No one even called me to say Happy Birthday. These bitches are something else,* I thought. Disappointed, I went home to celebrate by myself. Hell, I could've saved the money I paid Brenda to keep Zeta overnight.

Even Brina was missing. I'd been calling her for several days and still hadn't gotten a call back. *Damn! What a birthday,* I thought.

That evening, Londa showed up with two, huge beautifully wrapped boxes from Nordstrom's.

"What's this?" I asked.

"Open it and see."

When I unwrapped them, I almost cried. It was a Jay Godfrey wide leg jumper with matching shoes.

"It's from all of us," she said, kissing me on my cheek.

"Oh my God. It's gorgeous. Someone must've helped y'all no -dressing bitches pick it out, I said, holding it up so I could inspect it.

"You got that shit right. It took all of us to pay for the

bitch, too," Londa said laughing.

"I thought you guys forgot about me."

"Girl, please. No one forgot your birthday. Vicki had to run some errands but she's going to meet us at the club. Get dressed and I'll be back to pick you up at nine."

Dressed and ready to party, I called K-Dog to see if they wanted to go out with us, but he said they couldn't because they were out of town. I was so mad at him. I had talked with him at least two times the day before and he never mentioned anything about having to go to New York. Deciding not to make a federal case out of it, I told him I loved him anyway and I would see them when they got back.

Moments later, Londa arrived to pick me up. When I walked outside and heard her loud ass car, I shook my head 'no'. I was looking way too hot to ride in her piece of shit car and I told her so. It pissed her off a little but she knew I was right. When I walked over to my car and said, "We're driving this right here," her mouth dropped.

"Here, you drive," I said, handing her my key.

"No problem!"

"So, where are we going again?"

"Would you just sit back and relax. We'll be there soon."

We pulled into the parking lot of a club not far from my house.

"What are we doing here, I thought this was a private club," I said.

"It is, but it's open to the public tonight."

When the attendant saw Londa, he quickly ran to the car and took her keys.

"Where is he going with my car?"

"He's going to park it. It's called valet parking, girl-friend."

"Bitch, I know what it's called," I said with anger. "I ain't dumb."

"Well, excuse me, Miss Zsaset. But can you do me a favor?" she said.

"What?"

"Stop asking so many got damn questions."

When we walked up, the doors to the club were opened by two guys who had strange looks on their faces. It was like we were walking into a trap. Well, we didn't walk into a trap. I did. I walked right into a room full of people yelling, "SUR-PRISE!"

My heart skipped a beat and then I let out a heavy sigh as I covered my face. It was a surprise birthday party for me. Everyone was there. My friends from work, Quan, K-Dog, some other random neighbors that we befriended and some of my brother's friends. They even arranged for my girl, Sheba, to come up to Richmond and celebrate with me but Brina was nowhere in sight.

The first thing I did was wrap my arms around Sheba's neck. "Girlllllll, you know I love you, right!"

"Happy Birthday, Zsa! You didn't see this shit coming did you?" She grinned from ear to ear until I asked my next question.

"Where's Brina?"

She shrugged her shoulders.

Her expression confused me. It was a look of worry added with disappointment. I couldn't figure out why she hadn't returned any of my calls, and had now missed my birthday party. Something was terribly wrong but I played it off, and ran over to hug K-Dog. I was glowing and it was all because of him and his unrelenting generosity. I could tell by the look of the place it had cost a pretty penny, but knew he sure wasn't on the decorating committee.

The club was so beautiful. There were floating candles on each table, and chilled bottles of Veuve Clicqout lined the bar. The buffet was packed with buffalo wings, potato salad, chilled shrimp, and deviled eggs; all of my favorite foods. Anyone who knew me, knew that eating was my favorite pastime.

After singing happy birthday to me, people got up and made speeches. I held back the tears listening to Sheba's dedication to me.

"Zsaset is the true definition of a real friend. I love you, girl. Sky's the limit!!" she said, with tears, while raising her glass. Of course, her speech about friendship made me think of Brina again.

Everybody toasted and cheered. Suddenly, loud clapping roared through the room. I looked in the direction of the ruckus with attitude and took a deep breath when I spotted Yaya grinning with a head full of burgundy weave. She was wearing a hideous, metallic-pleather jump suit with a pair of cheap pumps. With all the money she was getting, I still couldn't understand why she always looked so tacky. I looked towards the door wondering where security was so they could escort her ghetto ass out before she ruined my party. She looked at me, winked her eye and snatched the mic out of Sheba's hand. *How did she even know about the party,* I thought.

"Ahhhhh, that was such a nice speech. Now it's my turn," Yaya said, grabbing a glass of champagne off the waiters tray with her other hand.

"What up, errrbody? I would like to make a toast to my girl Z, too. You know she very good at what she do. We have so much in common. And we actually share a lot of things including some juicy secrets! Don't we, Z?" she asked, holding up her glass.

"What the fuck is this bitch doing here?" I whispered with a fake smile to Londa who was standing next to me.

Everybody looked around, wondering if the toast was over. They realized it wasn't when Yaya busted out laughing then said, "Let me stop being fake. I'm about to tell y'all some shit about the real Z! But first I have a gift for you, Zsa." She handed a small unwrapped box with a card attached to the top of it. Open it. Show'em what I gotcha, girl!" Everyone was staring at me, so against my better judgment, I opened it.

First, I read the card. *'I guess you could use another one of these',* it read. I had no idea what the card meant so I opened the box. I almost shit in my pants when I saw a black Beretta like the one I used to kill the guys in Mosby Court. I quickly closed the box and attempted to get Yaya out of there.

"DJ, drop that beat," Yaya said, yelling in the mic as she walked away from me. The DJ started playing an instrumental version to Biggie Smalls 'Big Poppa'. "Two brothers got bodied, by a nobody. She thought nobody…."

I was about to die right there in the middle of the damn dance floor when that bitch said that. Thank God for K-Dog. He told the DJ to turn the mic off and turn the music up while O.B grabbed Yaya and escorted her out the door before she could say another word. I was so over this bitch. K-Dog was not about to let her ruin my day so he told me to go back to my party. He would make sure Yaya didn't bother me again. So, after two shots of tequila, that's what I did.

Then there was my birthday present from my brothers. I wasn't sure what else to expect at this point, as my stomach was in knots and I felt a panic attack coming on. *Bring it on*, I said to myself.

As the DJ started spinning a mellow tune, out of the corner of my eye, I noticed an impeccably dressed woman with a sharp pixie cut step out onto the stage. *No, it can't be*, I thought as I scanned the room for K-Dog.

K-Dog often talked about growing up in New York with Mary J Blige, my favorite singer of all time. Of course, I could not believe my eyes when she began swaying to the mellow beat and walking over to where I was sitting.

I screamed over the loud music like a deranged fan and sang every lyric along with her. The entire room was packed to the brim with family and friends and everyone was going crazy. *These dudes really loved me*, I reflected.

Afterwards, we all posed in a picture with her and, of course, she took a photo with the birthday girl herself. I was in heaven and I could tell everyone else was feeling good, by the smiles on their faces. This was sure to be a birthday I would never forget and a beautiful moment in our lives.

I Shoulda' SEEN HIM Coming

• • •

The rest of the night was off the hook. I drank one drink after another at the venue and I became so out of control. It didn't matter to me how much of a fool I made of myself. After all, it was my birthday and I deserved to have fun.

After my party, everyone headed to my house for the after party. Strangely, O.B and Quan said they had some important business to take care of, and wouldn't join us. Something weird was going on but I couldn't put my finger on it.

Of course, when we got to my house we were hungry as hell, devouring burgers and fries before falling to sleep. Sheba, K-dog, and I slept in my bed and everyone else slept wherever they could. I stepped on a few of them because there was nowhere to walk. They were so drunk, they didn't even feel it.

When I finally settled down for bed, I thought about how wonderful my party was and how lucky I was to have my friends. I texted Brina, once again before closing my eyes.

Once again. No response.

I attempted to allow thoughts of Ryan being with me soon fill me. It had been a great night but my gut told me tragedy would strike me soon.

twenty-two...

The next morning greeted me and everyone else with a major hangover. We were all fighting over my last few Aleves. Once the apartment was cleared, I took a quick shower in hopes it would wake me up. After I threw a pair of sweats and a t-shirt on, I went downstairs to fix me and Sheba something to eat. I guess the smell of the turkey bacon cooking got Sheba up out of the bed.

"This is what the hell I'm talkin' bout, hunty," she said, looking in the pan.

"It'll be ready in a minute."

As I was finishing up breakfast, I could hear K-Dog talking on the phone as he walked down the stairs. I could tell from the conversation some drama was going on. He kept talking about making sure they stayed strapped.

"Who you talking to?" I yelled.

"O.B and Quan. They just pulled up," he said as he opened the door and walked outside.

"Girl, I can't believe you still that nosy. Stop worrying about what the hell they doing and make me my damn plate. I'm hungry," Sheba said laughing.

"Bitch, do I look like Celie to you?" I asked. "Make your own plate."

I pulled out a plate and handed it to her. She was making

her plate when she noticed my cell phone vibrating. I suddenly thought about Deonte and why he hadn't been blowing up my phone.

"Zsa, your phone ringing."

I walked over and saw it was Mrs. Smith. "Oh shit! She must've made a decision," I said.

"Who?" Sheba asked.

I raised my hand to tell her to stop talking while I answered the phone. I took a seat at the table and began to speak. I noticed she wasn't as cheerful as I was. My first thought was the police had contacted her but I hadn't been arrested so that was just hearsay.

"What's wrong?" I asked when I heard the tone of her voice.

"Well, Mrs. Jones, I was all set to let Ryan come live with you but there's a problem."

"What's the problem?"

"Ryan told me that he didn't want to go."

"What do you mean he doesn't want to go?" I asked, confused.

I was in complete shock when she told me my son didn't want to have anything to do with me. Mrs. Smith asked that I give her some time to see what Ryan's issues are with me. I asked her if I could speak to him but she said she didn't think it was a good idea. She didn't want Ryan to feel like we were ganging up on him.

She assured me she would have him call me in a few days when things calmed down. I was devastated and being hung-over didn't help. My own child didn't want to live with me. He didn't even want to see me. Sheba, who was standing next to me during the whole conversation, started to rub my back as I cried.

While my mind was trying to settle down from the shocking news Mrs. Smith gave me, I got hit with bad news again. Detective Berry called and told me there was a warrant for my arrest.

My heart nearly stopped.

"What are the charges," I asked?

"Murder in the first degree. Now I'm going to give you the chance to turn yourself in, or I can come and get you."

Even though a lump had formed in my throat, I remained quiet and glossy eyed for a few seconds before speaking.

"Well, if you have a warrant, then how 'bout you just come get me!" I screamed, sick of his bullshit.

"Oh, I will, young lady. I have two witnesses that say you were there.

Again, I knew he was baiting me, so I flipped him off in my mind and remained silent.

"Miss Sassy Pants, for your information, the witnesses are solid. Do the sisters Lina and Yashika Hollister ring a bell?"

I froze.

Then allowed him a few more words before I cut him off.

"What? Wait a minute! " I said, jumping out of my chair. I knew right then; I'd pretty much given myself away.

I slapped my fist in my hand as hard as I could, while trying to wrap my head around Yaya and Lina being sisters. I knew there was something up with Lina's devilish ass. O.B and K-Dog were so sure Lina was loyal. She even pretended to act offended when K-Dog mentioned that the detective name dropped her in the shooting. That was the only reason she was allowed to stay in our circle, but everything was coming to-gether for me now. For months, I couldn't figure out how the police and Yaya knew about the shooting but it was clear who the snitches were now.

I slammed my phone down and ran outside to tell K-Dog, O.B, and Quan. Sheba followed me so she could be all up in Quan's face.

"Y'all are not gonna believe what just happened!" I screamed, out of breath. I started crying so hard I literally couldn't speak. I took a deep breath as K-Dog hugged me and tried to calm me down.

"The detective called and told me they have a warrant out for me. He said they have two witnesses now, Lina, and her sister Yaya."

When I dropped that bomb, you should've seen the looks on their faces. It was the look of absolute panic, confusion, disbelief and shock; Everyone except for O.B. His ass looked like he knew all along, although he tried to play it off.

As they tried to make sense of the news I had just given them, I noticed Ms. Brenda and Zeta parking and getting out of the car, while a compact car with dark tinted windows drove up slowly. As the guys consoled me, I cried hard with blurry vision and a snotty-nose.

I needed to get myself together to think clearly. Life was about to change at that very moment. If it had been any other day, I would've been on point, alerting my brothers, somehow. That day I wasn't. I had been hit with back to back bad news so I didn't react fast enough when I saw the guns pointed out of the car windows towards us.

Immediately, I became speechless, searched for Zeta, and attempted to duck for cover. Just like a movie, we all looked at each other and tried to part ways in an attempt to dodge any and all bullets headed in our direction. Every man for himself. Before I could even warn my brothers, deafening gunshots rang out.

The dudes were packing semi-automatic weapons. I knew because K-Dog taught me a lot about guns and which one you use to take a mothafucka out. These mothafuckas were not playing. They planned on taking us out as three dudes hung out of the windows of the black Charger. The driver tried to keep the little car steady, while going around the bend of an apartment complex.

On the ground, I could not account for my brothers.

It all happened so fast, was everyone dead?

Still in shock, I thought, *these assholes wanted us dead but little did they know, there was one way in and out of our complex and had I not been hit, I would have lit their asses up. Matter of fact, we all would have.* I rested for a while longer, not even caring what happened to me and if the shooters came back for more. I could not move a muscle and the site of the bullet wound was on fire, burning a hole in me. I wanted to die.

Minutes later, still in a complete daze and lying on the concrete, I searched for Zeta. There was no sign of her or Ms. Brenda, but I could see that Sheba, K-Dog, O.B and Quan were also on the ground. Nobody was moving but me.

"One of y'all mothafuckas move, got damn it," I cried. Nobody even so much as flinched.

The pain from the gunshot I suffered was excruciating and I began to whimper, almost like a child. I could feel the blood draining from my body as I turned to see Cindy running towards us with what looked like a cell phone. I silently prayed that an ambulance was on the way and Ms. Brenda would have enough sense to keep Zeta safe.

Then everything went black.

I Shoulda' Seen Him Coming *Part 2*
In Stores March 2015

Also By Danette Majette

CHECK OUT THIS EXCERPT
FROM
MISTRESS LOOSE
By: Kendall Banks

Chapter 1

Forty minutes into my fuck session, I thought Maceo was giving me a break; instead he carried me to the bed, laid me flat on my back, threw my thick thighs over his shoulders and began digging in again. I couldn't take it. I began to wiggle from underneath him, trying to escape. I attempted to back my body against the headboard, squirming like crazy. No matter what I did though, the dick was there waiting for me. It wouldn't let me escape.

Maceo grabbed me by the throat with one hand and applied pressure as he looked down into my eyes. I wasn't scared though as I looked back into his. Shit, I liked it. It intensified the moment. It almost felt like I was being raped or like he was literally *taking* my pussy from me without authorization. I loved it. There was no feeling like it. I'd never experienced loving that good even though I'd been with at least two hundred men. Maceo's sex game had gotten crazy over the last few months. Something strange was definitely going on with him.

As Maceo choked me, he fucked me like a wild savage. His hips repeatedly thrust back and forth in a vicious rhythm with a few of his dreads dangling in my face. His dick repeatedly entered and exited. My pussy muscles squeezed and tightened ending with a vicious clamp.

"Fuck me harder, Daddy," I begged.

He did just that. "Jassette, is this my pussy?" he asked me.

"You know it, Daddy. You know it. Now fuck me, harder!"

Since we'd been at it for nearly an hour, I was totally winded. I had bust several nuts already with Maceo finally preparing to bust *his first*. He pumped harder, deeper and faster as I watched his muscle-bound frame go to work. My Mandingo was ready.

"Cum for me, Daddy," I begged him. I wanted him to be happy. I needed him to embed in his mind how my pussy made him feel and how it forced him to cum better than any other chick. "C'mon, Daddy. Cum for me."

Looking me in the eyes, he finally did. He then collapsed on top of me with his dick still inside me. As he lay there, I wrapped my arms around him firmly against my body like he was really my man. The two of us just laid in the darkness in silence.

Maceo finally got up, turned on the light and grabbed his iPhone from the nightstand. He'd turned it off just before we started fucking. As he messed with his phone, I rested the side of my face in the palm of my hand and admired his chiseled body.

Maceo was 6'4" and a solid 255 pounds with a golden brown complexion. Perfection in my book; especially with those solid, muscular arms. His stomach held a sculptured six pack that no other nigga could rival and his eyes were an exotic shade of root beer. As he listened to his voice messages, I surveyed his gorgeous body, of course my eyes eventually made their way down to his dick. Although it was now limp, it was still thick, long and hanging low. I could even see thick veins slithering from the base of it to its humongous mushroomed head.

"Shit," Maceo said and began to dial a number. He then placed the phone on speaker and pulled his dreads into a ponytail while we both listened to the phone ring. Seconds later, I heard that one particular voice that always annoyed me these days…

Rena's.

"So why was your damn phone off this time?" Rena asked; anger evident in her whiny ass voice.

I sighed in annoyance, laid on my back and closed my eyes.

Bitch, was all I could think.

"It was charging," he told her.

"Don't fuckin' lie to me, Maceo. Why the fuck was it off?"

"Rena, I just told you it was charging."

"Where are you?" she blasted.

"Handling some business."

"I didn't ask you *what* you were doing. I asked you *where* you were doing it."

"Rena, don't start with a million fuckin' questions."

I sighed louder than before then reached for my cell phone from the nightstand.

Hearing me sigh, Maceo quickly made his way to my side of the bed, knelt down by his jeans and grabbed the metallic plated gun sitting on top. He then pointed it directly at my head, and whispered with total seriousness, "Shut the fuck up."

My body tensed at the feel of the cold steel pressed against my skull. My nipples hardened at the thought. I wasn't sure if he would actually squeeze the trigger but I didn't want to take any chances. I shut the fuck up just like he told me.

"Somebody told me they saw you hugged up with another bitch," Rena blasted.

"They're fucking lying," he told her as he stared down into my eyes then licked my left nipple.

"They ain't got no reason to lie, Maceo."

"Yes, the fuck they do! I keep telling your ass to quit listening to them air-head ass friends of yours. They don't have a good man in their life. They don't have nobody taking care of them like I'm taking care of you so they want to fuck up your relationship."

Maceo finally took the gun off of me. Angry at him, I climbed out of the bed, grabbed my purse and headed for the bathroom. Once inside while continuing to listen to him and Rena's conversation, I pulled out my Galaxy S instead of my iPhone. The Galaxy was my bat phone. That was the one I used to do my dirt. It always stayed on vibrate instead of ringer.

"Maceo, I'm getting sick of you lying to me," I heard Rena say as I began to type out a very important text.

"So, you gon' believe them hoes over me?"

Silence.

Looking at the bathroom door and ready to shove my phone back into my purse if Maceo appeared at the door, I waited for the conversation to commence. It finally did.

"Are you?" he asked.

Maceo's voice was already deep enough. Yet it had gotten deeper with extra rage added to its tone.

"I don't know," Rena said, sounding confused.

As they continued talking, I sent out the text and smiled. "Let's see how your slick ass wiggles out of this one," I whispered, while stuffing the phone back into my purse and heading back out into the suite thinking the text would mix things up a bit.

"So Rena, you think I'm with a bitch or something?" he asked her with confidence. "Is that what it is? Would I have you on speaker phone if I was with another bitch?"

Silence.

"Baby, I love you. I don't want anybody else but you. Alright?"

The thought of these two fake ass love birds killed my spirit. With Maceo's back turned to me, I quickly snapped a picture of his entire naked body from the back. I smiled when I was done knowing later I'd upload that ass to Instagram and Facebook. Quickly, I entered the bedroom again and rushed up behind him. He turned and gave me the evil eye.

"Alright," she answered but with reluctance. It was obvious she didn't quite believe him. But without solid proof she had to accept his word. "Well, what are you doing?"

"I told you; handling business," Maceo said with ease.

"Like what?"

"You know I don't talk on the phone, Rena."

She sighed.

"Look, I'll be home in about an hour. I love you."

"I love you, too," she said quickly.

He hung up and then headed for the bathroom. As he rushed off, I followed him. Just before he reached to turn the shower on, I asked, "How long is this shit going to go on, Maceo?"

"How long is *what* going to go on? Don't be a fuckin' nag."

My hands were now on my voluptuous hips as I spoke. "*This*. You and her.   Me and you."

"Wait, hold the fuck up. What are you trippin' on? You already know what the fuck is up. Rena is my wife. She's the mother of my child. You knew this from the start."

"I know that but..."

"But nothing. You know your damn position. Play it and don't worry about everything else. You get what you want, right?"

I froze for a second then let my eyes glance over my perky D-cups...the ones Maceo had paid for. The ones he spent eight grand on just a few days after I mentioned that I wanted them. I then thought about my flat abs and how much it cost Maceo to get all the fat sucked from my midsection. As seconds passed, I finally shook my head in frustration; more upset with myself more so than him. He was right. I knew my position and I had been playing it well- for over two years. I was the sideline chick...the chick who got all the benefits without getting the man. All of that was cool in the beginning. Now though, I was beginning to catch deeper feelings for Maceo. I wanted more.

"What are you shaking your head for?" he asked sensing my disappointment.

"Because I'm sick of being just your fuck toy."

Looking at me like I was crazy, he said, "So, what are you expecting...me to leave my wife or something?"

"I don't know what I'm expecting. But I want more than this."

"Look, Jassette, you're going to have to take this thing how I give it to you. Plain and simple as that. No negotiating."

Damn, his words were harsh. Shaking my head again, I said, "I don't know why I let myself get wrapped up in your cheating ass. When Monae first hooked us up, she told me to watch your ass but I didn't listen."

Laughing, he said, "First off, Monae shouldn't give anybody advice about a man. Secondly, cheating ass? Jassette, you knew I was a cheater from the jump. You knew I was married from day one. You said it was cool the first day we met. You saw the ring. You pursued me. Shit, ain't that why we're here right now?"

"Still." I sighed.

"And if I'm a cheater and you *knew* I was a cheater, what the fuck type of female does that make you? Don't try to look down on me because we're sinning differently."

I couldn't say anything. He was correct.

"You said you could handle this shit," he continued. "Can you or not?"

"I can."

"Then we're done with this conversation."

So he thought. My head nodded but my devious mind shifted off to another place. I wanted much more *of Maceo* and *from Maceo.* I wanted what Rena had. I wanted his child and his heart. And I was going to get it. No matter what it took.

Chapter 2

While Maceo showered, I got lost in my thoughts about the situation. I thought about the many men I'd always played second to. For some, I didn't care, they got what they wanted, and I did too. But with Maceo, there was something special about him; his swag, the way he talked, the way he handled himself. I knew we were meant to be together.

Besides, Maceo was a major boss in the streets. He was well-respected and had clout all over the city of Atlanta. He didn't carry himself like a thug but was a beast in the streets. Being smooth was his trademark, keeping his swag on high. I wanted it to be known that *I* was his woman and *not* Rena. With those thoughts running wildly through my head I quickly picked up my phone and uploaded Maceo's naked picture of the back of his body to Instagram. Of course I added my outlandish hashtags. **#badbitch #Illtakeyourman #goodpussy #moneyovereverything #youcantbeme.**

I wasn't sure if Rena followed me or even knew anything about my Instagram page. I knew Maceo didn't. He wasn't into social media and would go ballistic if he ever found out about my foolery. My hope was that someone worthy, even a few of Rena's friends would one day recognize my mysterious pics of Maceo even though I never showed his face. I wanted someone to tell her. I wanted the heat. I craved the drama. Then she'd leave him for sure. I had even tagged one of Rena's friends

@QueenBootylicious a few times hoping she'd check my page. We both had lots of pics in common showcasing the fancy gifts men had bought us, or places we traveled. I didn't like the bitch at all and definitely didn't like any of her pics...I just wanted her to know I fucked with Maceo.

Moments later, I heard the shower shut off. Maceo appeared butt naked, dick swinging, making me horny all over again. As I watched him rub lotion all over his body, I told him to come here.

He ignored me, and simply said, "The suite is rented for the entire night. You can stay or leave. If you're leaving, wait about fifteen minutes after I leave. A'ight?"

I didn't answer. I had an attitude with him.

"A'ight?" he asked more sternly.

"Yeah," I responded miserably. "But I want you to come here for a minute."

Maceo slipped his jeans on, reached into his pocket and pulled out a thick stack of hundred dollar bills. "No, Jassette. You come here."

Remaining in bed, I crawled over to him. When I reached him, I slid my legs underneath me and sat on my knees. I wanted my tits to talk to him subconsciously. He gave me a crazy look then counted out two thousand dollars. Again, he looked me in my eyes and tossed the two stacks toward the ceiling just over my head. The two of us stared at each other as the bills rained down around me onto the bed. He then kissed me; taking away my anger and frustration with him. As we kissed, I placed my hands on his shoulders. I loved the feel of his body. My nostrils also took in its nourishing smell.

"God, I love the way you smell," I told him as I rested the side of my face against his chest wanting to take in as much of his body's scent as I could.

I never knew why but something about the smell of a man always did something to me. Smelling them was now a habit of mine. I couldn't help it. And above any other man I'd smelled, Maceo's scent was definitely the most memorable.

There was something different about it. It mesmerized me.

My hands then traveled down to his dick. I wanted more of it. "Do you really have to go, Daddy?" I asked.

"Yeah, you heard the call. If I don't get home, it'll be World War 3 around my house."

Fuck all of that, I thought to myself. *Why would I give a fuck about his household*? I didn't want him to leave. And whatever I needed to do to make him stay, I would. Besides, I needed as much time as possible so the person I texted earlier could get in position. Manufactured tears began to well up in my eyes. "Maceo, just stay with me for tonight," I said meekly and with puppy dog eyes. Damn I didn't want to fuck up my $250 dollar lashes on a crying stunt. This needed to be worth it. "I promise I won't ask you again, Maceo. I just need you tonight."

Wiping away my tears, he said, "You know I can't do that, Jassette."

I dropped my head.

"What's wrong?" he asked.

"Just one of those nights. I still miss my parents. And being around you helps me through it."

The words were lies and truths combined. Yes, I still missed my father at times since the accident seven years ago took his life. But this wasn't one of those moments. I was just trying to tug at Maceo's heartstrings to make him stay. The truth was my mother was alive; even though I'd told Maceo she was dead. I had to do that for fear that my mother would meet him, realizing I was messing with a married man. My plan was to tell Maceo the truth the moment he divorced Rena and married me.

In all honesty though, the last thirty minutes in the hotel room with Maceo had sent me into my misery. He was the only person who could snap me out of it. Since my father's fatal accident, I didn't fool with my family too much. We were all cursed and no one truly wanted to face that fact but me. My oldest sister even took her own life because she realized it. And now my relationship with my youngest sister was practically non-existent, leaving me with only a handful of friends in my life.

Suddenly, I began crying uncontrollably and tugging at Maceo's jeans wildly. I wanted more of him. There was no way I would take no for an answer. Before long, Maceo gave in. At first, he tried to console me telling me that maybe I needed counseling to help get over my parent's death. Then he stuck his tongue inside me, making everything okay again.

On my knees and with my ass up in the air, my face buried itself in the pillow. Muffled moans, groans and other sounds I had no idea I could make escaped my mouth. I couldn't help it. Maceo was behind me munching on my asshole like it was his last supper. I mean, I'd had my asshole eaten out plenty of times by some skillful niggas but Maceo was definitely the best. The nigga was going absolutely hard.

"Ohhhhh, shitttt," I moaned into the pillow.

Maceo's tongue went deep inside my tight hole and was twisting and turning restlessly. As it did, he made sounds as if he was eating a steak. He also began to slide two fingers into my pussy, which was now soaking wet. He worked them in and out repeatedly while massaging my clit with his thumb. Damn, I wanted to tap out. The feeling was *super* intense.

"Mmmmmmm," Maceo moaned as he feasted on my tight brown hole, refusing to let up.

As Maceo did his thing, I reached underneath myself and began to play with my nipples. Both of them were hard as rocks. My fingers did a freaky dance and a nasty rub over and over again. I loved how it felt.

Maceo spread my cheeks with his hands and went deeper than before as if he hadn't gone deep enough in the first place. I couldn't believe how long his damn tongue was. It was damn near touching my spine. As he worked my asshole, he finger fucked me harder while working my clit faster. The change up made me play with my nipples more fiercely than before. The pleasure was increasing. My entire body could feel it.

"Fuckkkkkkk," I moaned into the pillow.

An orgasm was coming. I could feel it building up. I could feel it nearing. He must've felt it to because his mouth and tongue seemed to grow fiercer. They seemed to grow relentless. As they did, I let go of my nipples and gripped the sheets, bracing myself for the intensity of the upcoming orgasm. I knew it was going to be a big one. Sure enough, it was. It erupted so relentlessly my body trembled and both my pussy and clit grew *super* sensitive. Wanting to lay on my stomach and recuperate for a second, I attempted to but Maceo wouldn't allow it.

"Bring that ass back here," he demanded as he grabbed both my hips forcefully and positioned himself so that his raging erection pointed directly at my pussy. Before I could react or say anything, he was deep inside me.

"Oh, shit!" I screamed, slamming the palms of my hands down on the bed and shaking my head.

"Take the dick, bitch!" he ordered me as he snatched me by my twenty inches of weave so hard I thought my neck snapped. He then wrapped my hair around his hand once so he could have an excellent grip. "Take all of this dick, bitch!"

"Yessssssssss!" I yelled.

He slapped my ass so hard it stung causing me to yelp. He smacked it again even harder. I loved it. As he did, he plunged deeply into me. I could feel the nigga in my muthafuckin' chest.

"Ohhhh, Maceoooooo," I moaned. "I loveeeeeeeeeee your ass!"

Maceo's dick was just as thick as it was long. I could feel it spreading and widening me. I mean, the nigga's dick was about as hard as one of those dill pickles I used to eat as a kid. It was huge. Plus he knew exactly how to work it.

"Fuck me, Daddy!" I yelled.

Over and over again he plunged inside me. I could hear my pussy making wet sounds as he worked it. He then began to tease me by taking the entire dick out and putting it back in. As he did, the air and suction made my pussy make farting sounds.

"Harder," I begged.

"You my bitch?" he asked, continuing to tease me.

"Yessss," I told him.

Forcefully snatching me by my hair even harder than before, he demanded, "Say that shit loud then!"

"I'm your bitch, baby!" I yelled.

Slapping me on the ass, he said, "What?"

"I'm your bitch! Your ride or die! I swear I'm your bitch! I'm never leaving you!"

Keeping a hold of my long tresses, Maceo got up, led me across the hotel suite to the wall and forced my back against it. Damn, I loved how dominating he was being. It made my pussy even wetter. He then let go of my hair and lifted me off my feet. My legs were spread around him. The bottoms of my knees were resting on his forearms. My eyes were looking into his. Then once again, he entered me.

"Damn," I said at the feeling and the position. I'd never been picked up and fucked against a wall before.

As Maceo worked me, my nails dug into his shoulders. Over and over again, my pussy rose to the head of his big dick and plunged down to the base of it. Each time, the thickness made me feel like he was going to split me open. I held on to him for dear life.

"You like it, Jassette?"

"Yesssssssss, I *love* it."

He pounded me like a pile driver. Once again, I felt another orgasm coming. This one felt more intense than the first one. Feeling its upcoming arrival, I said, "Maceo, you're gonna make me cum again."

He slammed me against the wall and fucked me harder.

"Oh, shittttt, baby!" I screamed. Suddenly, something happened that I'd never experienced before. Instead of cumming, I squirted. The feeling was crazy. I thought I was peeing on myself as my juices skeeted out all over Maceo's muscular stomach.

"Yeah, that's a good bitch," he said while continuing to fuck me.

The wetness made our skin slap and bang together much louder than before. The sound echoed throughout the suite. I wondered if the people next door could hear us.

I was surprised at Maceo's stamina. He wasn't easing up and was showing no signs of cumming. He'd now had me against the wall for at least twenty minutes and I myself was winded. I needed mercy, but he was refusing to give me any. Before long, I was *squirting*, once again.

"Aweeeeeeee shit!" I screamed as my juices released and Maceo's eyes rolled up into his head. The nigga was finally cumming. He held me hostage in that position for nearly a minute while he savored on the moment, then released me from against the wall. I was nearly weak. He could see it.

Kissing me softly, he said, "Jassette, I gotta go. For real."

He never gave me a chance to protest. He simply rushed off into the bathroom taking his clothes with him. By the time he came back out he was fully dressed and wouldn't even look at me.

"Maceo," I called over to him.

"Jassette, I promise we'll meet up this week, a'ight?"

"That's not what I was going to ask you."

"I said, later, okay?"

I nodded.

Kissing me again, he grabbed his keys and headed for the door. As he did, he said, "Don't forget; if you're leaving, wait fifteen minutes." Before I could blink he'd left.

As soon as the door closed, I hopped out of the bed and got dressed quickly. *Fifteen minutes my ass*, I thought to myself while getting dressed. If that nigga thought I was going to keep on playing the role of sideline hoe for too much longer, he had another damn thing coming. Throwing on my clothes only took a moment. After gathering up the money on the bed and stuffing it in my Hermes bag, I was out the door. Seconds later, I was dashing down the stairs refusing to wait on the elevator. In no time I was in the lobby just in time to see Maceo opening the door of his Range Rover. As he did, an expensive ass Bentley Coupe screeched to a stop right in front of it.

"Perfect," I whispered to myself as I walked out of the

lobby and quickly dipped behind a pillar.

"So, you think I'm fuckin' stupid, nigga?" Rena screamed as she jumped out of the car and made her way around the hood.

"What the fuck?" he asked in surprise.

"Yeah, I got a text, muthafucka telling me exactly where you were. Where's the bitch at?"

"Rena, what the fuck are you talking about? Don't make me embarrass you."

"I'm talking about the bitch you were with, nigga. Don't play stupid. I know she's here. I know you're here with her!"

"Rena, you're tripping!"

"Am I?"

"Hell yeah!"

As they argued, I looked at Rena. She was a gorgeous, tall redbone draped in Louis Vuitton and diamonds. Her hair was naturally long and had a silky look to it. Her skin was smooth and had no blemishes anywhere that I could see. Even if I had found a flaw the white, Bentley she whipped would've erased all of that from my mind. The price tag was two hundred thousand and plus some. Fuck that. I wanted what she had. I wanted her position.

Grabbing my purse tightly, I sashayed from around the pillar and out into the parking lot. Approaching Maceo and Rena, Maceo's eyes locked on me. There was surprise in them. Nervousness.

Dread.

Despite it, I continued towards him knowing he was scared I was going to blow him up.

"Where is the bitch, Maceo?" Rena demanded. "Where is she?"

His eyes quickly glanced from me to her and back again. I continued towards them with my eyes locked on him.

"I swear, Maceo, I'm tired of this shit!" she continued ranting, keeping her eyes on him.

I got closer and closer.

"Which one of these cars is hers, Maceo?"

Finally, I was directly behind Rena. "Excuse me," I said.

Turning around quickly, she yelled, "What, mutha-fucka?"

Maceo was looking at me from behind her with spite and nervousness.

Everything went silent for a moment.

Finally, I said, "I don't want any problems, Miss. Just trying to get by you so I can get to my car. My man is waiting on me."

With that said, I walked past her and winked at Maceo seeing relief fall over him. Shaking my head and smiling, I headed to my car while Rena continued to go off on her husband. Stepping into my Porsche and turning the key, I backed out of my parking space and headed for the exit. As I reached it and began to send Maceo a text, a black Camaro pulled into the lot and slowly passed me. The sight of the driver made me do a double take. My bottom jaw dropped. Fear filled my bones. Bile rose in my stomach. Suddenly, my cell phone fell from my mouth and into my lap.

"Nahhh, it can't be," my mouth muttered as my eyes now watched the car's taillights through my rearview. "It just can't be."

Continuing to watch as the Camaro found a parking space, and the female driver hopped out, I was at a loss for words. As she made her way across the lot and into the lobby, I knew seeing her wasn't a coincidence. The bitch wasn't back in town for a friendly visit. She was back in town to check off some names on her shit list...

A list that *my* name was most definitely on.

Damn…more problems.

Mistress Loose
In Stores Now

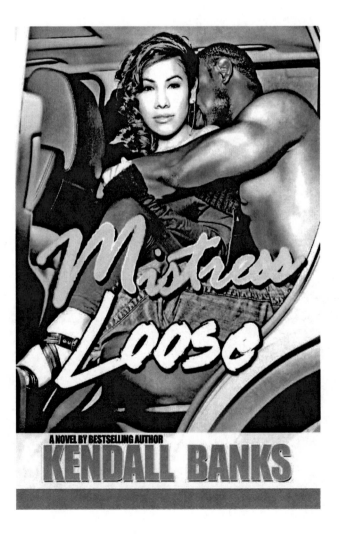

A NOVEL BY BESTSELLING AUTHOR
KENDALL BANKS

The DIRTY Divorce SERIES

PETITION FOR DIVORCE

The DIRTY Divorce 2
A NOVEL BY MISS KP

The Dirty Divorce Part 3
A NOVEL BY MISS KP

The DIRTY Divorce Part 4
A NOVEL BY MISS KP

www.lifechangingbooks.net

LCB BOOK TITLES

ABOUT THE PUBLISHER

Life Changing Books, more affectionately known as LCB, established in 2003, has become one of the most respected independent Trade Publishers amongst chain stores, vendors, authors and readers. LCB offers a variety of literature including, non-fiction, contemporary fiction, urban/street literature, and a host of other categories.

For more information visit us online at:
www.lifechangingbooks.net

Twitter: @lcbooks
Instagram: @lcbooks
Facebook: www.facebook.com/LCBooks

ORDER FORM

MAIL TO:
PO Box 423
Brandywine, MD 20613
301-362-6508

Ship to:
Address:

Date: _____ Phone: _____
Email: _____
City & State: _____ Zip: _____

Make all money orders and cashiers checks payable to: **Life Changing Books**

Qty.	ISBN	Title	Release Date	Price
	0-9741394-2-4	Bruised by Azarel	Jul-05	$ 15.00
	0-9741394-7-5	Bruised 2: The Ultimate Revenge by Azarel	Oct-06	$ 15.00
	0-9741394-3-2	Secrets of a Housewife by J. Tremble	Feb-06	$ 15.00
	0-9741394-6-7	The Millionaire Mistress by Tiphani	Nov-06	$ 15.00
	1-934230-99-5	More Secrets More Lies by J. Tremble	Feb-07	$ 15.00
	1-934230-95-2	A Private Affair by Mike Warren	May-07	$ 15.00
	1-934230-96-0	Flexin & Sexin Volume 1	Jun-07	$ 15.00
	1-934230-89-8	Still a Mistress by Tiphani	Nov-07	$ 15.00
	1-934230-91-X	Daddy's House by Azarel	Nov-07	$ 15.00
	1-934230-88-X	Naughty Little Angel by J. Tremble	Feb-08	$ 15.00
	1-934230820	Rich Girls by Kendall Banks	Oct-08	$ 15.00
	1-934230839	Expensive Taste by Tiphani	Nov-08	$ 15.00
	1-934230782	Brooklyn Brothel by C. Stecko	Jan-09	$ 15.00
	1-934230669	Good Girl Gone bad by Danette Majette	Mar-09	$ 15.00
	1-934230707	Sweet Swagger by Mike Warren	Jun-09	$ 15.00
	1-934230677	Carbon Copy by Azarel	Jul-09	$ 15.00
	1-934230723	Millionaire Mistress 3 by Tiphani	Nov-09	$ 15.00
	1-934230715	A Woman Scorned by Ericka Williams	Nov-09	$ 15.00
	1-934230685	My Man Her Son by J. Tremble	Feb-10	$ 15.00
	1-924230731	Love Heist by Jackie D.	Mar-10	$ 15.00
	1-934230812	Flexin & Sexin Volume 2	Apr-10	$ 15.00
	1-934230748	The Dirty Divorce by Miss KP	May-10	$ 15.00
	1-934230758	Chedda Boyz by CJ Hudson	Jul-10	$ 15.00
	1-934230766	Snitch by VegasClarke	Oct-10	$ 15.00
	1-934230693	Money Maker by Tonya Ridley	Oct-10	$ 15.00
	1-934230774	The Dirty Divorce Part 2 by Miss KP	Nov-10	$ 15.00
	1-934230170	The Available Wife by Carla Pennington	Jan-11	$ 15.00
	1-934230774	One Night Stand by Kendall Banks	Feb-11	$ 15.00
	1-934230278	Bitter by Danette Majette	Feb-11	$ 15.00
	1-934230299	Married to a Balla by Jackie D.	May-11	$ 15.00
	1-934230308	The Dirty Divorce Part 3 by Miss KP	Jun-11	$ 15.00
	1-934230316	Next Door Nympho By CJ Hudson	Jun-11	$ 15.00
	1-934230286	Bedroom Gangsta by J. Tremble	Sep-11	$ 15.00
	1-934230340	Another One Night Stand by Kendall Banks	Oct-11	$ 15.00
	1-934230359	The Available Wife Part 2 by Carla Pennington	Nov-11	$ 15.00
	1-934230332	Wealthy & Wicked by Chris Renee	Jan-12	$ 15.00
	1-934230375	Life After a Balla by Jackie D.	Mar-12	$ 15.00
	1-934230251	V.I.P. by Azarel	Apr-12	$ 15.00
	1-934230383	Welfare Grind by Kendall Banks	May-12	$ 15.00
	1-934230413	Still Grindin' by Kendall Banks	Sep-12	$ 15.00
	1-934230391	Paparazzi by Miss KP	Oct-13	$ 15.00
	1-93423043X	Cashin' Out by Jai Nicole	Nov-12	$ 15.00
	1-934230634	Welfare Grind Part 3 by Kendall Banks	Mar-13	$15.00
	1-934230642	Game Over by Winter Ramos	Apr-13	$15.99
	1-934230618	My Counterfeit Husband by Carla Pennington	Aug-14	$ 15.00
	1-93423060X	Mistress Loose by Kendall Banks	Oct-13	$ 15.00
	1-934230626	Dirty Divorce Part 4	Jan-14	$ 15.00
	1-934230596	Left for Dead by Ebony Canion	Feb-14	$ 15.00
	1-934230456	Charm City by C. Flores	Mar-14	$ 15.00
	1-934230499	Pillow Princess by Avery Goode	Aug-14	$ 15.00
			Total for Books	$

* Prison Orders- Please allow up to three (3) weeks for delivery.

Please Note: We are not held responsible for returned prison orders. Make sure the facility will receive books before ordering.

Shipping Charges (add $4.95 for 1-4 books*) $ _____
Total Enclosed (add lines) $ _____

*Shipping and Handling of 5-10 books is $6.95, please contact us if your order is more than 10 books.
(301)362-6508

CPSIA information can be obtained at www.ICGtesting.com
Printed in the USA
LVOW10s2155030415

433282LV00010B/85/P